KAWAND CRAWFORD'S

THE
BROOKLYN

D1519232

For information contact :
http://www.donkawand.com

Book and Cover design by Nicole Shephard
ISBN-13: -978-1544777818

First Edition: March 2017

10 9 8 7 6 5 4 3 2 1

DEDICATIONS

I would like to dedicate this to Kalief Browder, a young man who was arrested and sat on Rikers Island, a NYC jail for three years for a crime he didn't commit and when released finally committed suicide and every other young black man that's ever been profiled, abused, murdered or stripped of their dignity by a system designed to keep an entire race of people from achieving prosperity and happiness in this thing called life.

ACKNOWLEDGMENTS

First and foremost, I would like to thank God for blessing me with the talent to entertain and educate those through my writing.

I love my entire family for the love and support over the years. I would also like to thank everyone from Marlboro projects and Coney Island that I've ever broken bread with on the streets.

I would like to give an extraordinary special shout out to Tandrea D Lane and our beautiful and talented daughter Tanasia!

And last but not least I would like to shout out every caregiver I've worked with over the years including my current staff that's helping me live and enjoy my life to the fullest: Katarja Andrews, Evelina Beckham and Shanika Abrams!

PREFACE

The Brooklyn Konnection is a story that I was inspired to write after seeing the unjust killings of unarmed black men across the country because of the color of their skin. As a black man that was born and raised in the United States, I felt an obligation to use my writing platform to give my readers some insight on how difficult it is to survive as a black man in this country when dealing with a system that was strategically put together to destroy the existence of a race of people.

I grew up in Marlboro projects, only minutes from Coney Island and as a young black man was subject to brutal beatings at the hands of the police. It took me years to learn that the conditions I grew up in were designed for me to fail. It was absolutely challenging, but I am one of many that was blessed and lucky enough to survive, and be successful against all odds. -Kawand S Crawford

CHAPTER ONE

HEADQUARTERS

DECEMBER 2, 2014

CHUCKY

Crowd Screaming, **"NO JUSTICE! NO PEACE! NO JUSTICE! NO PEACE! NO JUSTICE! NO PEACE!"**

"Good afternoon everyone, this is Rafial Gonzales and we're live in lower Manhattan at the Mayor's office where thousands of people are gathered and protesting the brutal shooting of another unarmed black man in Brooklyn over the weekend by a white officer," Rafial Gonzales, the news anchor of NY 1 reported as my staff and I sat in my office with our eyes glued to the 40-inch flat-screen.

"Yo, Chucky, here comes your boy, that Italian cat just like you said!" Shondu, a childhood crimey of mines that grew up in Lafayette Gardens housing projects, shouted as he walked into the Brooklyn Konnection Headquarters.

"Good-lookin', brother Shondu. Okay, everyone out my office and look alive. This could make or break us. Everyone knows what they're supposed to do right?" I asked everyone inside of my storefront office on Nostrand Ave, just a few blocks from Marcy projects where I grew up at.

The two ladies and three fellas committed to my cause nodded their heads yes and filed out of my office, one by one just as I instructed while I waited for the Brooklyn Borough Pres. to enter my headquarters. After spending 20 years in a penitentiary, I'd become a new man; one dedicated to helping educate and uplift black people in my community instead of the brutal drug dealer I used to be when I was a young man.

I'd spent the last year trying to stop black on black crime but what happened over the weekend might change my mission and the thoughts running through my mind. I stepped into the doorway of my office and noticed Michael Calzone, Brooklyn's Borough President and the man next to the Mayor storming through the front door with two huge well-tanned Caucasian men dressed warmly in black wool trench coats following closely behind.

Michael Calzone, a short cocky Italian cat I went to John Dewey High School with was now the Borough Pres. and the backbone to my movement. He helped with my early release and assisted with setting up The Brooklyn Konnection, a nonprofit organization whose mission is to assist convicted felons like myself to adapt back into society as productive citizens. In return, these felons would go out on the streets with me and work to change the thought process of these young gang bangga's out here killing one another over neighborhoods and streets that the government owns.

I was expecting this visit but not so early on a Monday morning. Michael had a nice tan as if he'd just come off the beach even though it was the beginning of winter and you could see the frustration on his face from a mile away. It didn't complement the rich looking beige pea coat draped over a dark blue pinstriped three-piece suit. My eyes were stuck on his bright yellow tie when he stopped just in front of me.

"Chucky, Chucky, Chucky! We need to talk! I'm taking a lot of fuckin' heat from the Mayor on this one. I need your fuckin' help with this one buddy," my old friend strongly expressed while giving me a strong handshake.

"Tracy, see if these gentlemen want some coffee or something while I'm meeting with Mr. Calzone," I suggested, referring to the two men accompanying my old friend.

"Okay, boss!" Tracy, my ride or die chick, responded with a smile on her face.

Tracy had grown up in Bayview houses out in Canarsie and was not only my assistant but my go to lady with anything pertaining to my life! We met under some crazy circumstances but she turned out to be loyal and someone a brother could count on. Whenever she wasn't working for MTA (Mass Transit Authority) from 4 p.m. to midnight as a conductor, she helped with the organization.

She was a short chick when I went to jail but had grown into a beautiful 5'7" tall, slim, and sexy lady whose long legs I adored watching move through my office. Her dark mocha chocolate complexion resembled coffee without milk and her smile could light up a dark room. I glanced at her legs while she walked away and Michael stepped into my office after I slid to the side and gestured for him to go first.

I followed him into my office and after closing the door, he quickly spun around and cut straight to the chase like the man he is. There is no beating around the bush with Michael, something we had in common.

"This fuckin' shit over the weekend is fucked up, Chucky! I need you to talk to the protesters and calm them down before shit gets out of control. I know you're trying to help the community but we can't have people killing cops and rioting!"

"It's already out of control! You didn't see them bullet holes when you came in that I need to get fixed? And you're right. We can't have people killing NYPD's finest but you're wrong about rioting. The people are tired of marching and me preaching peace!" I snapped back.

"Come on, Chucky… I didn't come here to fight with you. I know you hear the rumors about this new gang, what are their names? Bitch Murderers… Bitch something retaliating. Do you know these assholes and can we stop shit from getting fuckin' bloody?"

"Yeah, I might. And there called Bitch Killers but from what I've been hearing they are well organized and a different breed. They're nationwide and spreading quickly through Brooklyn like cockroaches. These boys are smart. Real tight-lipped about the leader. If I can get to him then maybe I can do something. But don't hold me to it."

"Well listen! Do what you gotta do because if not, I'm gonna have to shut this operation down. I went out on the limb for you. Get this thing under control!" Michael demanded and I lost my cool.

I grabbed his little ass by his $1000 Italian suit with both hands in order to make sure I had his full attention. With my teeth gripped together tightly, I aggressively whispered, "NO! You fuckin' listen to me! Don't come in here threatening me after what I've done. You and I go way back and the only difference is our skin color. The both of us know that I wasn't supposed to do 25 to life but one of us became the Borough President and another one spent his time in lockup beatin' his dick for recreation. Do you know what it's like to spend five years in the hole? Do you know what it's like not to be with a lady or see your family like you want for over 20 years? Don't come in here threatening me! Do we understand each other?"

"Okay, Chucky, I didn't come here to skirmish with you. But this gang, Bitch Killers, needs to be talked to and fast. Killing a cop is not only going to be bad, it's going to be terrible on your community and neither one of us wants that." Michael responded with a much lower tone than moments ago, and I turned him loose.

He straightened up his suit and began to button his coat as we both stared at one another sending threatening subliminal messages with our eyes. Michael's father was a well-known made man in the Gambino family, one of New York City's most powerful Mafia organizations. To put it bluntly, they were well-connected with the politicians and some of the most ruthless men within the underworld of criminals. They are infamous for corruption, murder, and extortion; just to name a few.

Michael was a tough young kid, like myself, who I'd met in high school and although, most of his family didn't like black people, we became extremely cool. We got into some serious trouble, trouble that his family was able to get him out of while I took the rap. I spent most of my life in the mountains in upstate New York and miles from the city I'd grown up in. Michael and his family owed me because I had something on them that would ruin not only Michael but his entire family.

MICHAEL

I was furious when I stormed out of Chucky's office realizing that I might've lost a friend. Chucky might be the one that calls the shots in his neighborhood but I was the borough Pres. and I called the shots in Brooklyn. He'd been gone for over 20 years but the way people treated him, you would have thought he'd been running this operation a lot longer than six months.

Chucky came home acting like a new man, someone that wanted to help educate and uplift black people in his community but rumor has it, he was behind a different level of crime waves, one that included extortion.

Chucky spent the last year convincing people that he was helping to fight black on black crime but what happened over the weekend might change the way he operates. Although, Chucky looked dapper in his bow tie and expensive suit, deep down he was still nothing but a thug and he was forcing me to get down in the mud with him.

"Have a nice day, Mr. Calzone," Tracy, a pretty dark skin lady with long legs that he'd met a while ago on her knees, said as I briskly walked past her.

I nodded my head and kept it moving. Chucky had made a lady out of her. She cleaned up pretty well but once a whore, always a whore.

Although, he was out of prison, I had shared enough with Chucky to ruin me and my family. I owed him but putting his hands on me was crossing the line.

Once outside, I quickly spun around and cut straight to the chase. I turned to Jackie, my right-hand man who also handled my dirty work.

"Listen, make the phone call. It's time I put Chucky back in his place!" I ordered and knew at that moment there was no turning around. I had created a monster and one I would have to put down like a wounded horse.

CHUCKY

Michael Calzone's family's wealth was built on murder and extortion but that shit didn't faze me not one bit. Thoughts of how Michael and I met occupied my mind after he stormed out of my office knowing that I was going to be a problem.

Michael was a senior at John Dewey High School and I was a young freshman when we met and after the terrible altercation we'd just had, I couldn't help but to reminisce on the first confrontation we had that not only brought us closer but had us both feeling like we could trust one another.

We were students at John Dewey High School, a prestigious Institute in

Bensonhurst that I was accepted to because of my High IQ. I was extremely intelligent in intermediate school and one of my teachers suggested I take an entry exam to get into the school for students who have displayed excellence in academics. It was a place for the best of the best and although, it was predominantly white, I had no problem fitting in.

Even though it was an opportunity that my mother encouraged me to pursue, I ended up bringing my Bedford-Stuyvesant hustling ways to what I saw as a new spot to make a dollar. It was just before the Thanksgiving holiday that a few preppy looking white dudes rolled up on me about getting their hands on some cocaine. I think because I was black they assumed I knew how to get my hands on some good shit and they were right. By the Christmas break of my first year, I was in the Coke business. I was selling $20 bags for $50 and the bathroom was my place of business.

One Friday, I was in the bathroom meeting with skinny Sal when things got a little funky.

"How many you want?" I asked Sal, one of my best customers and a junior majoring in finance. "Give me two… I got three papers due by Monday and I really need something to keep me up all weekend." Sal added after answering my question.

Most of the students like Sal used cocaine to stay up all night studying for exams. Finals were coming around and things were picking up. I removed my knapsack which was hanging on my right shoulder and placed it on the bathroom sink while Sal complained about an Economic class. He was talking like he had taken a hit of something already as I went into my knapsack and pulled out a little plastic bag that had $1000 worth of cocaine prepackaged.

8

"Well, this right here should do the trick," I responded while passing him two small packages of cocaine.

Sal passed me a $100 bill which I quickly slipped into my pocket before stuffing the plastic bag of Coke back into my knapsack.

"Thanks a lot, man! I needed this, dude," he responded with a smile before turning and stepping swiftly out the bathroom.

I turned my back to the door and heard it open and close when I decided to pull all of my money out of my pocket and count it. "100, 200, 250," I was counting out loud when I heard the bathroom door open and close again and it startled me. I shoved the dead presidents in my pocket, flushed a nearby urinal as if I was using it, and walked back over to the sink to wash my hands. While standing in front of the sink, I noticed through the mirror that two big white guys, that look like they were on the wrestling team, were walking up behind me.

"Hey there boy! Whatcha doin' in here?" The taller and heavier looking one with a case of bad acne on his face asked after I finished washing my hands.

"Washing my hands. What does it look like?" I boldly responded before laughing at his foolish ass question as if he was stupid.

"So, you're some kind of comedian, huh? Hey, Lenny! He fuckin' thinks he's fuckin' Richard Pryor," he responded and they both started laughing. "Well, then tell us a joke, boy," the other one named Lenny followed up.

9

I looked around confused as if he was talking to someone else before saying, "Boy! I'm not your "boy". My name is Charles Washington but you crackers can call me Mr. Washington," I shot back standing firm and boldly.

"Lenny, you hear this fuckin' guy? This fuckin' nigga got balls on him. Are you fuckin' selling drugs in our school without our permission? Are you fuckin' crazy or fuckin' stupid? Nothin' goes on in here without us getting a piece of the action." The bigger one with the pimples scolded me while moving his neck from left to right, similar to a boxer moments before a fight.

"Wrong guy. I don't know what you're talkin' about," I lied before taking a step back after noticing Lenny, the quiet one, making a fist.

"You just said your name is Mr. Washington, right? Charles, the dope boy from the hood. You're the right fuckin' one all right."

I was surprised that he knew who I was so after the rude introduction, I confessed and they went straight into the business of trying to extort me.

"Fuck the small talk! We want a thousand dollars a week if you're gonna be selling dope to our friends," Lenny finally spoke out loud and confidently.

"Pay you a thousand dollars a week or what?" I quickly asked before he took a swing at me.

I dipped swiftly to the side and his fist brushed across my shoulder before I slung my knapsack, hitting him in the face. I then launched a hard blow that landed on his cheekbone that wobbled his legs but didn't put him out. He was reaching out to grab me as his legs wobbled and his friend sucker punched me to the side of the head. The aggressive attack demanded my attention. It all happened within seconds and I was fighting with them both when someone else entered the bathroom. My back was up against the wall as we all stood with our knuckles up waiting for one another to make the next move.

"WHAT THE FUCK!?" A short and well-dressed white dude yelled when he entered.

"WHO THE FUCK IS YOU?" I quickly responded keeping my eyes on the two in front of me.

"My name is Michael, Michael Calzone," the short guy introduced himself.

"I think your boys need a little help!" I shot back at Michael, who I immediately recognized as one of their friends.

My shirt was torn and the side of my face was stinging but I'd given them as much as they had given me. Lenny had blood coming from his nose and his face was red from the blow I delivered with my knapsack. The big fella's eye was red and swelling rapidly. My eyes were wide open and I was prepared to fight all three of them.

"So, you're some fuckin' tough guy or something, huh?" Michael asked while slowly approaching me.

"Fuck you and your friends. I'm not given up shit!" I shot back at Michael, who obviously had sent them in the bathroom first to test me.

I had both knuckles just inches away from my face as they hesitated to finish me off. The bathroom door swung open before we could mix it up again and it was a security guard. He dragged all of us to the Principal's office and every one of us denied the altercation. Michael and his friends kept quiet while I admitted that we were friends and just playing around. Michael was well known by the Principal for being a troublemaker and since I didn't admit that they were trying to rough me up, we all received a warning.

The next day, I went to school with a little 25 automatic expecting things to get worse but instead, Michael sat at my lunch table with me. I was the toughest black guy he had ever met and respected the fact that I wasn't no snitch. He sat across the lunchroom table from me and neither one of us broke the awkward stare as we began to bond.

Michael called his boys off of me and we came up with a deal that worked for the both of us. Most of his friends didn't like blacks and most of my friends cared nothing about them. We had a lot in common and neither one of us gave a fuck what other people thought.

"Hey, Chucky, your boy looked pissed the fuck off. Is everything good?" Shondu asked when he stepped into my office and caught me staring into space.

I heard him and slowly shook my head no before I explained how our mission of peace and uniting folks was about to turn bloody.

CHAPTER

TWO

PIMPIN' AIN'T EASY

ONE YEAR EARLIER - OCTOBER 2013

CHUCKY

I had a small brown bag of the only thing that I owned and couldn't leave behind when I walked out of 354 Hunter St., Ossining, NY.; a New York State correctional facility smack dead in the middle of the fall weather. Sing Sing Penitentiary had been my resident for the last 20 years, 3 months, and 5 days for a crime I didn't commit because I refused to snitch on who was involved.

I was approaching my 20th birthday when I lost my freedom trying to survive in a world designed to keep black men like myself fucked up! While I was in prison, I saw a lot of youngins coming and going only to return back shortly with longer sentences. Once you catch a felony it's difficult to survive once you're back on the streets. No one wants to hire a felon and once a grown man with very little education gets hungry, it can force a good man to do wicked things in order to eat.

Once released, I stood in front of the jail with my eyes closed, smelling the fresh fall air of freedom. I sucked it up for a moment before getting down on my knees and kissing the cool concrete ground before thanking God for blessing me with another chance at life.

I stood to my feet, looked back at the 30-foot concrete wall, and glared at the barbed wires at the top for a moment before turning and noticing a shining black limousine in my sight. There was a middle-aged white guy dressed in all black which appeared to be the chauffeur.

"Are you Mr. Washington? Charles "Chucky" Washington?" The soft-spoken man's voice sounded from a distance.

"Yeah, that's me," I responded curiously to the well-groomed white guy who knew my name.

He had a smile on his face. As I cautiously approached him, he introduced himself, "Well, my name is Jackie Salvatore. Mr. Calzone, an old friend of yours sent me to pick you up. Where would you like to go?"

I was a little hesitant at the friendliness of the driver when I asked, "He sent you to take me anywhere I wanna go, huh?"

"Anywhere you like. Mr. Calzone hopes you enjoy your surprise and he wants you to get in touch with him as soon as you settle in." Mr. Salvatore continued as he opened the back door for me.

I reluctantly stepped in and immediately realized that someone else was already inside.

TRACY

MOMENTS EARLIER

I was in the backseat of a luxurious limousine, restless as hell and sipping on some Peach Ciroc when Chucky's fine ass self-exited Sing Sing, a free man. His clean shaven, bald head was glowing from the brightness of sun shining on it even though it was a cool day and I couldn't help but notice the beauty of his handsome and unblemished face as he slowly strolled over to the car. His pretty brown complexion had me gently biting on my bottom lip as he spoke to the driver unaware of my presence. My eyes were glued to his face and his thick black eyebrows are what brought out the sexiness in his ass and just looking at him made my heart skip a beat.

I could hear them talking from inside as I waited impatiently to surprise my Bae.

"Would you stop running your damn mouth!" I mumbled out loud while Chucky questioned the driver.

I didn't ask any questions when Mr. Calzone called yesterday and asked me to ride to Sing Sing in his personal limousine to pick up Chucky. My Daddy was every bit of a boss man on the streets before he went to jail. His charismatic and smooth talking ass got him whatever it was he wanted and if that didn't work, he took what he wanted.

I watched his eyes open wide at the sight of me sitting in the back seat wearing a smile, a pink trench coat, and some matching 6-inch heels like he dreamed of in the letters he wrote me.

"Oh shit! Whatchu doin' here!?"

"Comin' to get my Daddy!" I seductively responded just before he leaned in and gave me a strong and firm hug.

"Aaah, it feels wonderful to be free. DAMN! You smell good as FUCK! Girl, let me look at you!" Chucky stated before sitting in the seat that was facing me and smiling like he had lost his mind.

I had my back to the driver and enticingly crossed my legs and placed both of my hands on my knees to give my man a tease of what he had asked for. He sat there grinning, shaking his head, and blinking his eyes to make sure that he wasn't dreaming.

"You're not dreaming, baby. You're free and I'm real. Come touch Mama again," I stated as I prepared to give him what he'd fantasized about for years.

Chucky just sat there shaking his head and my pussy grew moist when he spoke, "Pink coat… Heels…huh? Are you wearing what I think you're wearing underneath that coat?"

"That's for you to find out. Don't be scared to touch me," I whispered seductively before uncrossing my leg and prepping to display the main course.

As he gawked at me not knowing what to say or do, I began to reminisce about how we met only two months before he went to jail.

I was only 16 years old when this 25-year-old pimp nigga named,

Caesar, talked me into selling pussy to survive. I thought he really loved me but six months after we met, he started geekin' off that crack and heroin. Caesar could be really nice until he needed a fix and this particular night he was hurting pretty bad.

It was about two in the morning and Caesar had me working on Workmen Avenue, a hot spot for freelancing prostitutes in East New York. It was a couple quiet blocks in the back of Pennsylvania Avenue's White Castle and he was beating my ass after some fat white bastard complained about how I was giving him head. Sucking someone's dick was not my thing and it made me sick every time I had to; I didn't mind fuckin' for money but could never get used to a man sticking it in my mouth. That shit was just disgusting!

Caesar had me by my throat, squeezing tightly, and screaming in my face, "BITCH! HOW MANY FUCKIN' TIMES I GOT TO TELL YOU NOT TO USE YOUR MOTHER FUCKIN' TEETH!"

I struggled to breathe. "LOOK AT ME BITCH! LOOK AT ME!" Caesar continued before covering his teeth with his lips and moving his tongue around. "THIS IS HOW YOU DO IT BITCH!" He continued unable to scream at me.

I was crying and after making the mistake of looking him in his eyes, he punched me in my stomach, buckling me and causing me to clutch my stomach with both hands.

"AHHH," I sighed after he'd knocked the wind out of me. "Okay, Caesar, okay!" I pleaded as I wished that I was dead.

If Caesar knew how to suck dick so well why the fuck he didn't do it? Is what crossed my mind but never came out my mouth. There were times I did question if he was a switch hitter because he didn't mind me playing with his back door but I never asked. He was hard on us girls as if he really didn't like pussy, even though he was the one that broke my virginity. He kept me safe from the other vultures on the streets after I'd lost both of my parents and got tired of living in foster care.

Large drops of tears flowed freely out of my eyes and I tried desperately to stand back up and breathe when he slapped me across the face and yelled, "ON YOUR KNEES BITCH! YOU'RE GONNA GET THIS SHIT RIGHT TONIGHT!"

He unzipped his pants and reached in, "Stop fuckin' crying. And you better not get tears on my dick either! Wipe your fucking face and get this shit right, bitch!" Caesar continued with his half hard dick in his hand as I slowly got down on my knees.

It was around 2 o'clock in the morning and very few people were out when this car pulled up and came to a stop.

"Put your hands on me, you punk mother fucka!" A tall, slim brown skin guy with some jewelry around his neck shouted and he was already out the car, moving swiftly toward us.

Everything happened so fast and before I knew it this stranger had his arm around Caesar's neck. He grabbed Caesar from behind, catching him off guard and just in time. Caesar was clawing at his arms, his face, and trying to get loose as I watched his eyes bulging out of his head.

"Get in the car, ma... GET IN THE FUCKIN' CAR!" he screamed at me while he continued holding Caesar in a choke hold.

I was scared and didn't know what I was getting into but I was more afraid of Caesar. He always bragged about killing a bitch that owed him $20 and although, I was terrified, I remained loyal to Caesar for far too long. I'd finally grown tired of the shit he was doing to me and decided to take my chance with this fella and the clean-cut white guy sitting in the driver's seat. At first, I thought they were lovers when a bitch jumped in the backseat as instructed.

Caesar was going to kill me next time he saw me is what crossed my mind while I watched him get tossed to the ground.

"DON'T YOU EVER PUT YOUR HANDS ON A FEMALE AGAIN! YOU FUCKIN' HERE ME?" The stranger yelled before kicking Caesar in the face with the tip of his boot.

It was hard and made me turn my head briefly and when I looked back, Caesar had blood leaking out of his mouth. He tried to pull out a knife he had in his back pocket and it got him kicked and stomped on. He gave Caesar an ass whoopin' as if he had slapped his mama until his friend jumped out the car and made him get in.

"This punk ass got blood on my Timbos! I just brought these motha fuckas! FUCK!" He complained before turning to the back seat and asking, "You okay back there, baby girl? You too pretty for a nigga to be puttin' his hands on. My name is Chucky and this is my boy, Michael."

"He's gonna kill me…" I whispered nervously as he passed me some tissue to help stop the blood that was coming out of my busted lip.

"That bitch ass nigga ain't doing shit, baby girl! How old are you anyway because you look a little too young to be out on the streets whoring for some punk ass nigga!?"

They were both surprised to find that I was only 16 and had nowhere to go. I thought Chucky and his friend just wanted to have a good time but Chucky was every bit of a gentleman. He promised that he'd take care of me and that I wouldn't have to go back to Caesar. His friend dropped us off at Marcy projects where Chucky lived with his older sister and three nephews.

Chucky was a sexy chocolate manly man that didn't want anything from me, so he said. I felt comfortable with his sister in the house and that night he treated me nicer than any man ever had. He lived in the projects but the crib was nice as hell. Chucky gave me a T-shirt with the Notorious B.I.G. on it after I got out the shower and even slept on the couch that night and that's when I knew I'd met the man of my dreams. He was the first man I met that didn't want to fuck me and leave me.

It didn't take me long to find out that Chucky was a big-time drug dealer. He knew everyone in Bedford-Stuyvesant that was somebody and was very well respected. He had other bitches but I didn't mind because he treated me like royalty and there was nothing I wouldn't do for him.

Chucky's voice snapped me out of the moment when I heard him asking, "So let me see what you got on underneath the coat."

"Guess?" I toyed before slowly unbuttoning my coat.

"I'm thinking a sexy negligée or nothing at all," Chucky responded with a perverted smile on his face.

He was licking his lips and glared at me as if I was a T-bone steak ready for tasting.

"Oooh shit!" He stated before laughing once he noticed me wearing the Notorious B.I.G. T-shirt he'd given me the first night we met and nothing else.

"You was close," I stated before taking the trench coat completely off.

"Whatchu doin', girl?" He whispered like a little boy as I got down on my knees, crawled over to him, and began to unbuckle his pants.

"Shut up! I'm not a little girl anymore," I whispered before puckering my lips like Caesar had shown me and proceeded to give Chucky the blow job of his life on his first day out.

SHONDU

It was a few minutes after 3 PM when I finally made it to Marcy to pick up some change that this chick, Leticia, had when I noticed a couple young boys on the corner of Nostrand and Park Ave shooting dice. Every last one of them had plenty of paper in their hands and quickly turned when I pulled up and beeped the horn for Kendell, even though everyone calls him, K-hooly. Kendell is Chucky's nephew and wasted no time coming over to the car.

Chucky and I had known one another since PS 270 so his family was mine. While he was bidding, I made sure his sister, Phyllis, and her kids wanted for nothing.

"What's good, Unc?" K-hooly asked after placing both of his hands on the roof of my car.

"Just checking on you, Lil' nigga. Who was bussin' last night? Was that you?" I boldly questioned.

"Come ooon, Unc, you know how the streets be. Some nigga's from LG came creepin' through last night acting up so we put fire to their asses just like you and uncle Chuck used to do."

"Nigga's from my ol' hood? I just sold a couple of banggas to some cats out there… And me and your uncle wouldn't be out the next day without them hammers on us. We'd be on point, not throwing bones in broad daylight so that someone can catch us slipping." I said noticing that all of them had not even noticed me pulling up until I beeped the horn. I could have put at least two of them down for the count by the time they realized what was happening.

"Yeah, I be knowin', Unc, but yeah, some nigga from your old hood. A nigga named, Prince, tried to clap nigga's last night. You know we can't have that… And we got hammers on deck. I got the 40 Glock sitting on top of the back tire of this whip," he responded before using his head to gesture toward an old looking Buick parked near the curb.

"Oh word, Prince Maintain? You don't know this but your uncle and me grew up with that lil' nigga's pops. If he's anything like him, he'll be coming back for some blood. Ya'll lil' niggas be careful because you know the streets are not kind to anyone. You hear me?"

"Yeah, I be knowin', I got this, Unc. You raised me well."

"You know your uncle is getting out today? He should be out now," I responded looking at my watch and seeing that it was after three in the afternoon.

"Yeah, I know, moms told me he was all righteous and shit these days," he stated before a brief laugh.

"Look, your uncle and me broke a lot of bread together on these streets. He's a smart dude and knows the streets better than anyone. It's going to be up to us to help him make that adjustment. You hear me?"

"I gotcha, Unc… Whatchu doin' creepin' this early?"

"I came to pick up some change from Leticia and then I'm out. How's Mama Love?"

"That's what's up and mom's good. She doesn't get home from the plantation until after six, though."

"Okay, tell her I said hello and tonight I'm gonna bring you a bulletproof vest. And you wear that shit until I straighten them nigga's in LG. You hear me, lil' nigga?"

"Yo, K, I'm getting ready to spark this blunt," Tom Tom, one of Kendell's lil' soldiers hollered.

He glanced over his shoulder and barked out, "Nigga! You don't see me choppin' it up with my Uncle... Hold the fuck up with that! And yeah, Unc, I heard you."

"Well look, you be safe out here, nephew, and have your uncle, Chucky, call me as soon as you see him. If you need some hardware, get at me."

He gave me a head nod of approval before turning and bouncing back onto the sidewalk where his homies were. "Yo, PULL YOUR PANTS UP!" I yelled while shaking my head after noticing he had his boxers and half of his ass on display.

K-hooly reminded me of his uncle because he was popular with the ladies and he got them young boys in Marcy under his wing. The streets respected that lil' nigga similar to how everyone treated Chucky. It's crazy how these little motha fuckas are going through the same shit we went through back in the days. I tried to talk K-hooly out of the streetlife a few years ago but got nowhere. He was hell bent on being on the streets, so after a couple of months of trying to steer him in the right direction, I decided to school him on how to get it while staying free and alive.

There wasn't too much that went on in Bed-Stuy that I didn't know about, so after I got a call last night about the shooting, I had to come check on him and remind him to stay on point. Even though K-hooly could handle himself, this shit with Prince concerned me.

The boy's father, a well-known gangsta nicknamed, King Maintain, was a FUCKIN' PROBLEM! He gave Chucky and me hell! He ate off of sticking up drug dealers and gambling spots and was not afraid to draw blood if you didn't hand that shit over quick enough. That nigga definitely had a mean gun game because he was known to keep two banggas on him at all times. The only problem he had, which contributed to his downfall, is that he moved alone. He trusted no one and no one trusted him.

Chucky had enough of him after he robbed one of our drug spots on Gates Ave, between Tompkins and Troop, for about $13,000 in cash and close to 100 g of powder. It was Chucky's spot but Kaseem, a cat that ran with us, and I were responsible for making sure everything ran smoothly. Kaseem was inside of an abandoned building that we used as a spot and I'd taken a run to Kennedy's Fried Chicken for some hot wings. He fucked around and opened up the door thinking it was me when King Maintain pushed his way in and took what he wanted.

When I returned, I found Kaseem tied up and blood leaking from his face. King Maintain had pistol-whipped him and left him for dead. He was lucky to be alive. It was the first and last time King Maintain took something from Chucky.

Chucky had put 10 grand on his head and $5,000 to anyone that knew where he was hiding. Brooklyn was huge but very small when you're about that life. King Maintain's name rung bells just like Chucky's, except Chucky was loved. It didn't take Chucky long before he found out that King Maintain was fucking with this chick on Chauncey St., which was on the other side of Bed-Stuy, and all we had to do was wait until we got a call. Once that rabbit poked his head up out of the hole he was hiding in, we were going to take it off.

I was parking next to Leticia's building when I began to reminisce on the night we caught King Maintain slipping.

It was a cold Sunday night when Chucky got a call from Zenobia, a bitch he was fuckin' with that lived on Chauncey St. between Saratoga on Hopkinson Ave, whose sister was hiding King Maintain out in their parent's basement. Chucky had Zenobia watching his every move for about a week before this evening. She'd noticed that he'd sleep and hang around the house throughout the day and right before midnight he'd leave and wouldn't return until the sun came up.

This night, Zenobia had called Chucky and told him that King Maintain was in the shower and getting ready to leave the house. Chucky was no slouch and didn't like getting his hands dirty but for some reason, he wanted to be there. Chucky was the smart one out the crew and kept us afloat with the change and Kaseem and I dealt with the nigga's that disrupted our cash flow. And this nigga King Maintain had definitely disrupted our flow.

Chucky was across the street on the side where the two-family brownstone house was located, smoking a cigarette on the corner of Saratoga and Chauncy. Kaseem and I were on the other sidewalk of the one-way street laying low on the steps of PS 137, watching the brick house he was supposed to have been in. It was a cold, fall evening and very few people or cars were moving up and down the block while we waited patiently for Chucky to whistle when dude was coming out. Zenobia was going to hit Chucky just before King Maintain left the house.

Kaseem was a live cat from East New York I met when I was locked up in the Navy Yard on a parole violation. He was from Miller Ave or Killa Miller is what they called it and was not afraid to pull the trigger. We were passing around a pint of E & J to keep warm when we heard Chucky sound off a double whistle. I took my last sip of the brandy, hurried up and put the top on, and slid it in my back pocket. Kaseem and I got up off the steps and began pretending to have a conversation when we spotted King Maintain coming out the house across the street.

This nigga was wearing a black leather jacket with a sweat hood underneath which he'd thrown over his head and pulled tightly before skipping down the flight of steps that would have him standing on the sidewalk. He kept his hands in his pockets and we knew he was strapped as he consciously surveyed the block from inside the gate that separated the house from the sidewalk where shit was about to get real.

Once he exited the black gate surrounding the house, he stopped and looked to the left where Chucky was standing smoking a cigarette with his back to King Maintain. He then glanced across the street at us and we pretended not to notice him. He was acting paranoid and we must have spooked him because he started up the block in the direction away from Chucky. I looked over at Chucky who nodded his head for us to follow him just before disappearing around the corner.

Chucky had planned for this move and had already decided that if he didn't come in our direction, Chucky would run around the block and catch him at the other end of the street. Chucky was on the move as Kaseem and I shadowed close behind from across the street. Halfway up the block, King Maintain peeped us on his tail. He started stepping a little quicker as Kaseem and I pulled out banggas at the same time.

I quickly cut between two parked cars and made my way into the street where I bent down so he couldn't see me because of the parked cars. Kaseem was right behind me with the 357 Magnum in his hand. Before we could get up on the sidewalk, King Maintain stopped and instantly displayed two big handguns when he noticed that we weren't across the street anymore. I could see him looking for us as I began to creep up on the sidewalk.

Kaseem stayed in the street and once King Maintain laid eyes on me, he immediately popped off two quick shots; one from each bangga. Bang! Bang!

I threw two back from the 9 mm Beretta before ducking behind a car. I peeked up over the car and fired three more shots at him before he disappeared between two cars and out of my sight. He was making his way into the streets and I stepped up on the sidewalk to get a better view.

"YO, KASEEM!" I screamed before bending down to look underneath the cars to see if I could spot this nigga's feet while listening to him exchange gunfire with Kaseem.

I spotted his boots several cars down and as I went to stand up, I heard someone screaming out loud in pain. The gunshots had stopped and I maneuvered back into the street where King Maintain and Kaseem were shooting at one another. King Maintain was running in the middle of the street toward Hopkinson Avenue, the nearest corner, and my homie was curled up on the ground between a couple of cars.

"YO, KASEEM! OH SHIT! KASEEM!" I yelled while making my way to him.

Blood was leaking out of his chest after he rolled over on his back with his gun not too far from him. King Maintain had put my man down. Seeing my homie on the ground struggling to breathe hit me hard and as much as I wanted to help, I couldn't because murder was on my motha fuckin' mind!

By the time I picked the 357 off the ground, King Maintain had turned the corner and disappeared out of sight.

Bang! Bang!

I heard two loud shots pop off which made me stop in my tracks. With the 9 mm in one hand and the 357 in the other, I slowly crept around the corner afraid of what I was about to see. When I turned the corner, Chucky was standing over King Maintain, who was lying face down with his body trembling.

"YO, KASEEM IS HIT… LET'S GET THE FUCK OUTTA HERE!" I yelled.

Chucky looked at me then back at King Maintain and fired three more rounds into his back.

Bang! Bang! Bang!

"WHO IS IT!?" Leticia, a chick from the projects that sold dope for me, yelled after I knocked on her door and images of that cold but fatal incident faded.

"IT'S SHONDU, OPEN THE DOOR!" I screamed back through the steel door.

A sense of excitement ran through my body knowing that my nigga, Chucky, was going to be back on the streets. Things had changed and I wondered how he would adjust to this new breed of pill poppin' nigga's as I listened to the loud sound of the deadlocks opening to Leticia's door.

CHUCKY

"Listen here love. I gotta go," I informed Tracy before stuffing another piece of crispy bacon into my mouth.

Damn it felt good to taste some real bacon instead of that plastic shit they fed brothers in the penitentiary.

"Okay, babe. Love you and I'll see you later," Tracy responded before giving me a quick kiss on the lips and following me to the front door.

I paused in the doorway, turned around and Tracy was glowing. I could tell she was in good spirits and a brother was feeling grateful that she was still in my corner.

"Look at my baby looking all handsome and professional!" Tracy stated while brushing something off the shoulder of my suit jacket.

I leaned in and put my tongue inside of her mouth one last time before leaving. Tracy had the hips and thighs of a big girl that my hands could not get enough of. She had gained some weight over the years but it was in all of the right places. She was a little insecure with the small pouch she had just above her waist area but it was expected from a lady in her 30s with two kids. Tracy was too busy running the streets up until a few years ago so the kids were currently staying with their father.

Tracy worked for transit as a train conductor and making pretty good change for herself. She'd come a long way since the time I found her on her knees trying to make a living off of selling her young self for some no-good rat. She was renting out the basement of a private house just off of Flatlands, a very quiet block in Canarsie, a relatively decent neighborhood in Brooklyn. It was just the environment I needed to make the proper adjustments.

Our lips were locked tight as last night's pleasurable moments flashed in my head. Tracy had pleasured every inch of my body with her lips and I couldn't get enough of her, but I had to go.

"Damn, girl, you and them soft ass lips," I complimented after licking my lips and getting a taste of her cherry lip gloss.

Tracy turned her head slightly away and giggled as if I was embarrassing her.

"Stop it, Chucky, go ahead and take care of your business and stop trying to make my pussy wet before I end up not going to work. I'm going to cook you some lasagna before I go to work for you eat tonight. We got a lot of catching up to do so take care what you got to and I'll see you later," Tracy stated before I gently stroked the side of her face with the back of my fingers.

I'd been gone for a long time so just touching a woman at this point in my life was something I was still getting used to. I'd gotten into a lot of trouble the first couple years I went upstate and quickly got labeled a dangerous inmate. Therefore, my visits came with special protocols. I was not allowed any personal contact and was confined to a glass partition with a phone on each side for us to communicate. I wanted to marry her but she wanted to wait until I got out of jail. She wanted a real wedding, a romantic but pleasurable honeymoon night and I didn't blame her.

There was a newsstand on Rockaway Ave directly in front of the entrance to the L train that I needed to take to downtown Brooklyn. I needed to meet with an old friend that I was hoping was going to help me with my transition. Michael Calzone, an Italian cat I met in high school was now the Brooklyn Borough Pres. and owed me his life.

Once I was on the train, I began flipping through the pages of the New York Post newspaper when an article on my old friend, Michael, cleaning up the streets of Brooklyn had gotten my attention. He'd been in office for a year and was looking good in this picture of him and the Mayor. I admired the picture after reading the article and was confident he was in a position to help with the growing crisis of black on black crime.

Shortly after reading the good work Michael was trying to implement, the next story just solidified my ambitions to make a difference. It was a story about a young man that was murdered in cold blood earlier this morning and it happened to be in my old stomping grounds, Marcy projects, and my sister, Phyllis, and her kids came to mind. She knew I was getting out of jail but I spent the evening with Tracy getting some much-needed pampering and special treatment. Not to mention I wanted to tell Tracy my plans first because I could count on her being brutally honest. I'd shown her the ideas I'd written down in a notebook over the last two years in confinement. It was a detailed plan that required someone in politics with a lot of power to help make it happen.

I couldn't help but shake my head in disgust while reading the article of the slaying of another young boy in Marcy projects. Marcy was my hood and a part of me was sure that he was probably the son of someone I might know. I continued to read article after article and for every good story, I read there were three bad ones.

It was about 9:45 a.m. when I finally arrived at Michael Calzone's downtown Brooklyn office on Court Street.

"Good morning, my name is Jessica, can I help you?" The young looking redhead behind one of the three desks said when I walked into the ground floor office space that was set up like a politician's headquarters.

"Yes, my name is Charles Washington. I'm here to see Mr. Calzone. I'm an ol' friend of his." I stated as she continued to maintain her smile.

"Mr. Washington? Chucky?" She called out my nickname as if to make sure I was the same person.

"Yes, that's me," I answered before holding my hand out for her to shake.

She leaned in and shook my hand with both of her hands.

"Oh my God, it's nice to finally get to meet you. Mr. Calzone talks about the two of you all the time. He told me to expect you any day now. Give me one second, Mr. Washington." She stated before finally turning my hand loose.

Now, I've been gone for a long time but when she pulled her hands away it appeared that she was intentionally caressing the back of my hand. She never broke eye contact until my hand was freed and she began to make her way to a door just a few feet away from her desk.

My eyes locked on Jessica's small butt and the short one piece orange dress that stopped just above the back of her knees. I wallowed at the view until she disappeared.

"Hey, can I get you some coffee or a bagel or something," a young black fella with an eye-catching bright green bow tie and some eyeglasses with distinctive black frames asked.

He was dressed casually in an octagon sweater that matched his beige khakis and had all of the appearances of a college student.

"No, thank you. I'm good," I responded as the young fella just nodded and went back to the desk he had been sitting at when I entered.

I sized him up out of habit before looking around and admiring the well-decorated office that my old friend was running. My back was to the door that Jessica disappeared into so I didn't notice when she came out and called my name, "Hey, Mr. Washington. You can come on in now... it was nice to finally meet you!" Jessica concluded as I breezed past her in the doorway, catching a nose full of her sweet-smelling perfume.

She closed the door behind me and Michael was already standing behind his desk. He was wearing a huge grin and dressed in a very expensive looking suit. He quickly made his way from around the desk with both arms open.

"Charles "Chucky" Washington… Get the fuck outta here! Good to see you, ol' friend!" Michael excitedly greeted me as we approached one another in the middle of the brightly lit room.

We embraced one another like old friends and the hug he'd given me screamed love through my entire body.

"Good to see you, too. And thank you for the recommendation letter you wrote to the Board of Parole on my behalf." I said extending my gratitude after he turned me loose. "And you didn't have to send a limo to pick me up yesterday neither."

"What? Are you fucking kidding me, bro!? It's the least I can do for an ol' buddy. Not to mention I was hoping we could work together on fighting crime in this city. Hey, where are my manners? Here, take a seat. Make yourself comfortable." Michael offered before pulling out an expensive looking leather chair that was positioned in front of his desk.

I took a seat as he maneuvered back around the desk and sat in front of me. He placed his folded hands on the desk and leaned in, "Well, Chucky! It's definitely good to see you after all these years… Man, you look good! Tell me… what I can do for you before I tell you my ideas," Michael spoke with a smile on his face.

Michael looked the same as he did in high school except he had put on a few pounds and his slick black hair had some streaks of gray. Even though Michael was the Borough Pres., I knew that he was not flying straight. He always had his hands in something, let's say a little illegal.

"Yes you can," I responded before dropping three black and white notebooks of several things that I thought could help with black on black crime in the community. "I want an office like this. One that I can run an organization called "The Brooklyn Konnection" out of to help felons transition into society while getting them to help me cut down on some of the black on black crime."

That's how I started and I didn't plan on leaving until he reassured me that he would do everything in his power to keep me from going back to jail.

PHYLLIS

"Shondu, this is Phyllis. I need you to call me immediately. When I came out of my building this morning there was detectives everywhere and they had yellow tape in front of the corner store on Marcy Ave. Someone got murdered last night. Please give me a call! Kendell didn't come in last night and I'm kind of worried. Nigga, call me as soon as you get this message." I whispered through the phone trying not to allow the strangers on the train to ear hustle my conversation.

This is the third time I called this motha fucka and he ain't answer. There was no telling which one of his little whore's bed he was laying up in. I continued to pray that nothing happened to my son while wondering why my brother hadn't contacted me yet after all the shit I'd done for him.

My brother wrote me plenty of letters about how he changed and found Jesus but no one knew him like me. He was pure street since the day he was born and coming back to the same shit concerned me. Most of his friends were either dead or in jail, except for Shondu, and a couple others were actually strung out on dope. I was about to call Shondu's ass again when my phone began to ring. I looked at the screen, seen his name, and quickly answered.

"Yeah, nigga! Why haven't you been answering my calls? I've been calling you all morning. What the hell happened last night? I asked without giving him a chance to say hello.

He was the only one I could think of that would know what was going on in the PJs even though he didn't live out there. Although, he'd grown up in LG, he'd spent a lot of time in Marcy with my brother and was still about that life that kept him on top of what was going on.

"Hey, sis, sorry but I just woke the fuck up," He mumbled through the phone before yawning in my ear.

"Wake ya ass up, nigga! Put your dick back in your pants and tell me what the hell happened last night." I demanded through the phone while my eyes scanned around to make sure no one was paying me any attention.

The roaring sound of the train whizzing through the tunnel is what I relied on to help keep my conversation somewhat private.

"I'm not sure, sis, but I do have a couple of missed calls from Leticia around four in the morning. Let me give her a buzz and see what the fuck is going on and I'll hit you back."

"Okay, and did you hear anything from my brother?"

"Naaah, not yet but I'm sure I'll hear from him today. He probably spent the night getting his dick wet... Shit, that's what niggas do on their first night out the joint. Especially, after the time your brother just did. We might not hear from that nigga for about a week," Shondu commented and he did have a point.

"Okay, enough about what my brother could be doing, nigga! Call one of your lil' bitches up and get back to me. ASAP, nigga! Don't have me worrying about my son another minute." I stated before hanging the phone up.

SHONDU

"Hey, Shorty, can a nigga get something to eat?"

"Didn't I give you enough to eat last night? And don't be trying to get me out the room so you can call some other bitch! I heard whoever that was you were talking to... Don't try to play me like that, Shondu," Zenobia stated before crawling out of the bed with her smartass mouth.

"Come on now... I'm talking about some food," I responded before laughing. "And that was Chucky's sister, Phyllis. Some shit popped off in the hood last night and she's just concerned about her son." I explained briefly while she grabbed a T-shirt off the chair and slid it over her nude body.

"Yeah right, nigga, get your funky ass up out my bed and out my house if you wanna call one of your bitches! I know I'm not your girl but you ain't gonna play me like one of these wretched bitches you be fuckin' with," Zenobia barked at me before strolling out of the room with half the T-shirt sitting on the top of her ass.

I watched her pull it down past her butt cheeks before slamming the door and disappearing into the hallway.

"I'M NOT PLAYIN' WITH YOU, SHONDU! DON'T BE CALLIN' NO OTHER BITCHES IN MY HOUSE! AND DO YOU WANT SOME FRENCH TOAST BEFORE YOU GO?" She yelled from the kitchen as I began to hear the rattling sound of pots and pans.

Zenobia was more bark than bite and knew exactly how to stay in her lane. It's one of the reasons that Chucky liked her so much. Zenobia only fucked with a nigga like me because she loved a high profile nigga. Chucky and Zenobia had popped off a few times but I don't think it was serious, which is why we both felt no guilt when I ran into her a couple of months ago at this Hot 97 all white party on a yacht.

We had a few drinks and hung out the rest of the evening. She was wearing a white strapless fitted dress that stopped just above her knees and whenever we danced, she made sure to turn around and back that ass up on me. My hands were exploring her waist and when I noticed she wasn't wearing any panties, I knew I wanted to fuck the shit out of her!

What was supposed to be a one-night stand turned into months because Zenobia had the good-good between her legs and a part of me was hoping that Chucky had forgotten about her.

Even though she was popping shit, I hit Leticia up any motha fuckin' way to find out who got bodied last night. That was the only time they broke out the yellow tape and Lord knows I was praying that it wasn't my nephew. Leticia kept me posted about everything that went on when I wasn't around. Her phone had only rung one time before she answered and she went straight into telling me about the shootout last night that sent someone to the morgue.

"Hold the fuck up! Is my nephew okay? That's what the fuck I wanna know!" I said aggressively trying to get down to the point because Leticia could talk.

"I don't know! I haven't been outside yet. Them boys had me sleeping on the floor since 4 o'clock this morning. They were shootin' like crazy! I mean like 100 shots must've been fired. A bitch wasn't leaving the house until the sun came up." She explained.

"WHAT? Hit the streets bitch and find out what the fuck happened! Call me back ASAP, you hear me!? FIND OUT WHO THE FUCK IT WAS AND CALL ME BACK!" I yelled into the phone before hanging up.

I angrily snatched my pants up off the floor, dug my hand into the pocket, and pulled out a stack of greenbacks. I quickly counted out $500 and slapped it on Zenobia's nightstand next to my empty condom wrapper before getting dressed. I skipped washing my balls and headed to the kitchen where the aroma of cinnamon coming off the French toast had been coming from.

"Listen here, ma! A nigga gotta hit the block. I left some change on the nightstand for you. Get your cable cut back on and keep the rest for yourself," I said walking up behind her.

Zenobia had her back toward me and was flipping over the French toast when I grabbed her by the waist and gave her a gentle kiss on the back of her neck. Zenobia shivered before whispering, "Don't do that… And you could at least eat something before you go. I know you didn't have me cook this shit for nothing," She sarcastically responded.

"I'm sorry, ma, but I lost my appetite. Put it in the fridge and I'll heat it up later when I come back.

"Don't lie to me, nigga! You ain't coming back. I'll eat them myself. You go check on your nephew and your other little bitches and call me whenever you like, as usual." She shot back with her back still toward me.

There was nothing I could say because she was right. Even though I always said I would see her later, I never did. When I got outside is when it dawned on me that I had a missed call from Phyllis. After taking my phone out of silent mode, I called her back and she was already at work still wanting to know what happened but I had no answers.

"Look I'm on my way out there now to find out what went down," I stated to Phyllis who was beginning to sound like a nervous wreck.

"I think I'm gonna leave work early. Please call me back as soon as possible and tell me something. If something happened to my baby… ugggh! Shondu, hurry up and find out what the fuck happened!" She cried to me.

"No doubt… As a matter of fact, I got a call coming in now from Leticia. Give me five minutes and I'll call you right back," I said to Phyllis but she insisted that she hold on.

I didn't argue and accepted the incoming call and Leticia was crying hysterically. I could barely understand a word she was saying but it didn't sound good.

CHAPTER

FOUR

SAME OL' HOOD

CHUCKY

I was coming out of the Willoughby Ave train station on the G line for the first time in years and was still dumbfounded at how much had changed. The train station's appearance had me at awe as I exited from the underground station to the street. Shit was crazy and everyone I spotted seemed to have a cell phone, something Tracy said she was going to pick up for me sometime today. They were just becoming popular before I went away but now it seems that everyone had one stuck to their ear.

"Oh My God! Hey, Chucky! I heard you were home." A short heavyset girl that looked familiar said before stopping in front of me.

She appeared to be wiping her eyes with a tissue as if she had been crying when I reluctantly responded, "Leticia? Lil' T?"

"Yeah, nigga, stop actin' like you don't remember a bitch like me!" she shot back. "I know I've put on some weight but it doesn't stop anything."

We both started laughing because she looked like a butterball compared to the well shapely young girl I knew when we were younger but her attitude and confidence was intact.

"A yo, Chucky Chuck… Is that really you?" A skinny, old looking fella shouted that I quickly recognized as Cockeyed Marc.

We were about the same age but this nigga had the appearance of someone's grandfather. The alcohol and drugs had done him bad as he approached us throwing off a horrible stench.

"Now, Marc, you know it's too early in the morning for you to be drunk," Leticia criticized.

"Marc, what's good with you, my brother?" I swiftly spoke back with a smile on my face and ignoring the horrible smell.

"It's not too early for me considering I've been drinking all night," Cockeyed Marc joked and we all started laughing. "And I'm good, Chucky. Just trying to survive in this jungle. You be careful out here, man, these young boys are losing their minds."

"I'm good, Marc. Just came to check out the ol' neighborhood and check on my folks."

"Hey, why don't one of you lend an ol' playa a dolla or two," Cockeyed Marc boldly asked while scratching his right temple and struggling to keep his eyes open.

"Ain't nobody got nothin' for you to go get high with. You need to go take a shower or something and pull yourself together, Marc. Ain't nobody got time for this. Get outta here with that begging shit this early in the day," Leticia continued popping shots.

Marc was one of my best customers in my young days and I could feel his pain, so I quickly pulled out a five-dollar bill and slipped it to him.

"Oh, Jesus! Thank you, Chucky! Thanks a lot, Chucky! It's good to see you back in the neighborhood. The streets miss a cat like you."

Marc was smiling hard and staring at the five dollar bill as if it was a winning lottery ticket. It was at that moment that I noticed he was missing a couple of teeth. "No problem, just don't spend it all in one spot," I suggested before Marc did a little happy dance and skipped off, probably on his way to get a bag of heroin.

"Damn, you look good! You just missed your friend, Shondu… You want me to call him and tell him you're out here?"

"Shondu!? What's that dude up to these days and hell yeah, call that fool!" I requested as she continued talking while finding his number, "Oh, he think he's some kind of boss nigga out here. Tryin' to be like you. Do you remember Kim? Well, she calls herself Shahadah now. Her and your sister, Phyllis, used to be cool in high school. Her brother, Monty, committed suicide when we were younger," Leticia continued before putting her phone on speaker.

"Monty sister? I think so… little bit why?" I reluctantly responded after the mentioning of his name brought back a bad memory.

I remembered the incident with Monty very well because his death bothered me for years but couldn't quite put a face to who Kim was.

"Someone killed her son, lil' Billy this morning. He just turned 20 last week. Him and your nephew, Kendell, are good friends, I mean were. Your nephew reminds me so much of you when you was his age," Leticia continued while we listened to the phone ringing. The phone rung about five times before Shondu finally answered.

"Hey, Shondu, where are you? I got somebody here that wants to talk to you."

Shondu was my man, 50 grand and we ran hard on the streets. He was a good dude and loyal. After hearing my voice, he demanded that I stay put. Shondu was my dude even though we didn't stay in touch while I was up north. He'd done about five years but I never ran into him during my stretch. My sister kept me on point with some of the things that were going on but I knew Shondu would be able to catch me up with everything. We spoke briefly because he was on his way but it was good to hear his voice.

"So I guess you haven't heard?" Leticia asked before explaining to me how my nephew had been caught up in the life. The rumor was he was the target and her words pierced my heart. My nephew had no idea about what he was involved in. Leticia told me some stories about him that made me cringe even though it was nothing I had not done myself. What my nephew didn't know is that they had a jail cell with his name on it or even worse, a spot for him in the cemetery at an early age. I couldn't help but wonder how I would react if he was gunned down in cold blood.

SHONDU

Damn, my dude is home was all I was thinking about as I left Murray's Corner, a clothing store on the corner of Atlantic and Nostrand Ave. I had to grab my man a couple pairs of them True Religion jeans, a couple shirts, and a little somethin' somethin' for the feet. It was some shit that I should've done about a week ago when Phyllis first told me he was getting out but I didn't.

It was only right after all this nigga had done for me when we were younger that I help him get back into the swing of things. "Damn, it felt good to hear this nigga's voice," I mumbled out loud slamming my hand on the steering wheel. Just thinking about him sent me back into the early 90s when we were balling hard. Some guilt came over me about not staying in touch with him like I should have but I'm sure he understands how the streets work.

I was weaving through traffic on Bedford Ave, listening to this new joint by Jay-Z with a smirk on my face at the excitement of hooking back up with a real OG, the Black Don is what us closest to him called him, although, he didn't like the name.

It was a little after one in the afternoon when I pulled up on Chucky with my music blasting and caught him chopping it up with Shahadah. She was dressed in all black and had obviously been crying. I couldn't imagine what she was feeling after finding out that her son was murdered but it was the life he chose just like the rest of us. Death or a long time in jail was the destiny for anyone that hung out on the Avenue selling drugs and playing with them steel nigga killers.

"Hey, girl, I gotta go. Again, I'm sorry for your loss…" I heard Chucky saying to Shahadah after he spotted me pulling up on the side of a parked car. Shahadah was with another lady I'd never seen before who had her arm locked tightly with hers and appeared to be keeping her on her feet.

"Thank you, Chucky, I still can't believe somebody killed my boy! This shit got me fucked up!" I heard Shahadah responding to Chucky before she burst into tears.

The lady wrapped her arm around Shahadah whose legs were buckling and Chucky leaned in to keep her up.

The loud sound of a police siren and the flashing red and white lights in my rearview mirror startled me as a cop cruiser sped past me on an obvious call. They were out early and everywhere as Chucky approached the car.

"Get in, nigga… Let's get outta here because the block is hot," I said to my homie when he grabbed the handle to the passenger side door and quickly jumped in.

"AHHH, WHAT'S GOOD, MY NIGGA!" I excitedly expressed my love just before giving my long-time friend a pound and a hug.

"Shit, still trying to soak up just being home. I see the streets are still making young mothers cry. When is this shit gonna stop?" Chucky blurted out, fucking up the mood just before I pulled off.

"Yeah, man shit is crazy out here. Ain't too much change, just different players. How does it feel to be home? Got you some pussy yet?" I asked, shifting the conversation and we both started laughing.

"Come on, nigga. You already know. Remember my little shorty, Tracy? She was waiting for me in a limousine yesterday. Shit was crazy but that's why I love the hell out that chick!"

"Get the fuck outta here… The Black Don has returned," I said and we both started laughing. "I know that was one hell of a ride," I continued and we both started cracking up like old times.

"The best ride of my life," he stated and we started laughing again. "But yo, let me tell you some real shit. I thought them crackers wasn't gonna ever let me go. It feels good to be free, to wake up next to some pussy, and be riding with my homie up the Ave like old times. And you pulled up just in time. All of this police activity got a nigga paranoid and shit! So what's up with all of the fuckin' police?"

"So you telling me you haven't heard about last night?"

"Well, Lil' T told me a little something and then Shahadah…" Chucky paused for a minute and I can see him shaken his head out the corner of my eye. "Some little nigga's from LG murdered her son, huh?"

"Yeaaah man, they murked the little fella… And you saw Lil' T? I guess you see she's not so little anymore, huh?" I stated before we both started laughing.

"Yeah, she definitely put on some pounds. But what's this shit going on with my nephew?"

"We're going to meet up with your sister now and run up in the court building to see what's going on. He got snatched up last night in that bull shit! Yeah, him and his little friends have been actin' like it's World War III out this motha fucka! They've been beefing with some young boy's in LG for about a week." I explained to Chucky while he stared aimlessly out the window checking out the scenery. "These young fellas today don't have no fuckin' respect for life. But they know who to fuck with!"

"Yeah, I know. It used to hurt my heart to see them young boys come to the penitentiary for some dumb shit. Yo, this shit has to change." Chucky stated shaking his head in disgust as I filled him in on how his nephew was living.

"I tried to keep Kendell, I mean K-hooly is what they're calling him on the streets now, out the life but the boy is hard headed just like we used to be at his age. When I couldn't talk him outta taking that route, I figured I'd just school him on how to survive like you did with us."

"You can't teach that shit. It didn't keep me out the penitentiary. And now look at my nephew. Locked the fuck up for some bull shit!"

"At least he's alive. Remember what you always used to say, it's better to be judged by 12 than carried by six." I quickly reminded him of his infamous slogan.

"Yeah, but I got some plans for us. Big ones that're gonna make a difference. I'll tell you about it later. Yo, what the fuck is that?" Chucky asked as we passed the Barclay arena on Atlantic and Flatbush Ave.

Chucky couldn't believe how they cleared out enough space for the building. He then began to talk about some ideas he had for us to help save lives instead of contributing to taking them. It was something he talked about until we got to his sister's job and that's when I knew that the gangster that I once ran the streets of Brooklyn with was not the same nigga at all.

* * * * * *

CHUCKY
3 DAYS LATER

"Docket number 3468j... New York versus Eugene Hamilton... robbery in the second degree, possession of a firearm's, murder in the first degree ..." The court officer yelled out in the quiet courtroom filled with people.

"Mr. Hamilton, how do you plead?" The judge asked.

"My client pleads not guilty your honor," the middle-aged Jewish lawyer responded on behalf of the young man that looked no older than 18.

"Your honor, the people recommend that the defendant is remanded without bail. The defendant waited in the staircase for Roger Greene, a rival drug dealer, and robbed and murdered him in cold blood. The defendant fired 13 shots into the face and body of Mr. Greene before taking the money and jewelry off of his person's." The prosecutor spoke loud and firmly.

I watched and listened as the prosecutor and defendant's lawyer went back and forth for a moment before the judge remanded him without bail. Case after case a young black man came before the judge as we waited for my nephew to be arraigned. He'd been in jail for three days and, although, he only had a gun possession, my nephew was not new to the law.

I sat three rows back from where the prosecutor was with my right arm around my sister and Tracy holding my left hand. Every time a young black man came before the judge, the more I was reminded of a promise I made to myself to do my best to make a difference. I never thought I'd see the streets again in my life and prayed to God every day that if I ever did, I would use every ounce of strength to make some changes. I'd been a part of the street shit too long was what I was thinking moments before they brought my nephew out before the judge.

"Docket number 3415k... New York versus Kendell Washington... Possession of a firearm and resisting arrest!" The court officer shouted out.

Seeing my nephew delivered a sharp pain to my chest. Here I was sitting in Brooklyn criminal court, a building that I vowed to never visit again, praying that my nephew is let go. I could see the despair on the family member's faces that sat where I was and only imagined myself wearing the same expression. There was nothing we could do except wait for our loved one's faith to be decided by an old white man in a black robe sitting on a bench.

Every time a young man was remanded and sent back, there was a loud scream or outburst from his family who would eventually be escorted out. My sister, Phyllis, was strong but wanted me to be with her and I was more than willing to support my sister and nephew. It was the least I could do after she sat in court every day during my trial.

"Oh, My God! What did they do to him," my sister spoke softly but it echoed across the silent courtroom.

"PLEASE BE QUIET MA'AM OR STEP OUT THE COURTROOM!" one of the court officers yelled out in our direction.

I pulled my sister close to me because the court officers meant business. My nephew had a white bandage over his right eye as if he had been in a fight. I knew all too well how the NYPD operated when someone didn't cooperate. Even though it's been 20 years, I remember the ass whoopin' I received the day I got arrested as if it was yesterday. I spent two days in the hospital and weeks recuperating from broken ribs, not to mention my face was swollen in several different places.

I could feel Tracy squeezing my hand as I prayed for a good outcome for my nephew. The prosecutor and my nephew's lawyer went back and forth about bail until the judge ordered him to be held on $20,000 bond which was relatively obtainable compared to the rest of the decisions I'd heard earlier. They wasted no time rushing him out of the courtroom and I quickly got my sister out of there.

"Did you see what they did to my baby?" She complained once we were in the hallway.

"Yeah, they just roughed him up a little bit," I responded as if it was no big thing.

"$20,000! Chucky, I don't have that kind of money sitting around. What are we gonna do?"

"Don't worry, sis… We can go around the corner and find a bail bondsman and get him out for a portion of that. I'm home now… Stop worrying! Ima handle this." I promised while attempting to console her.

"Somebody needs to talk to his ass! Lord knows his daddy ain't shit! I can't do this by myself anymore, Chucky," my sister cried out and I was forced to wrap my arms around her.

She started crying when Tracy placed her hand on her back and whispered, "Hey, Phyllis, come on, girl. Stay strong, everything is going to be all right. You've got us."

Tracy then went into her bag and pulled out some tissue and we all made our way out of the building. It was drizzling when we came out shortly after 3 PM and Tracy was the only one with an umbrella. Soft drops fell on me as Tracy and my sister stood underneath the umbrella contemplating our next move. Tracy was doing her best to soothe her soul while I was in deep thought.

We'd been in the courtroom all day waiting for my nephew to come out. I couldn't help but wonder what was going on with this generation of young folks. It bothered me but I saw a lot of myself inside of each and every one that came out, including my nephew. The only difference is that during my time, most of us went to jail for drugs or robbery. These young boys are coming in front of the judge for murder and in some cases multiple murders. Life meant nothing to these young boys!

"Here, Tracy, take this and walk my sister to that spot across the street, J & J's Lounge, and get her a bite to eat and a drink to calm her nerves," I suggested after pulling some money out of my pocket and passing Tracy a $50 bill.

"You're not coming with us?" Tracy asked.

"I'll be over there in a few minutes. I'm going to run around the corner and holler at an ol' friend. Going to see if he can help me find a good bondsman," I responded before watching them both walk off.

I pulled my fitted hat down close to my eyebrows, placed my hands in my pockets, and quickly made my way around the corner to visit my friend, Michael. I hadn't heard from him in a couple days since I left him my ideas on how to help my peoples. I remember him telling me he was always in his office until at least 4 PM and I was hoping that today was one of them days.

CHAPTER
FIVE
CHUCKY'S FIRST TEST

MICHAEL

"Hey, Jessica, need you to clear my calendar next Tuesday morning. I have a very important meeting." I shouted to Jessica, who was in the other room.

"Do you need me to set up the meeting?" She responded before appearing inside of the doorway.

"Not at all. I got this one under control." I boasted before she turned and vanished.

The Mayor was putting pressure on me to do something about the increase in homicides that was going on in Brooklyn. We'd met earlier for lunch and he promised to give me whatever I needed to make it happen. I grabbed my jacket off the back of my chair and after slipping one arm inside, heard a knock on my door before seeing Jessica standing in the doorway with an unusual grin and blushing.

"Excuse me, Mr. Calzone, but your friend, Mr. Washington, is here."

"Well send him on in," I suggested while I finished putting on my jacket.

I'd just fastened the first button on my jacket when he entered my office and that's when the lightbulb went off over my head.

"Chucky, my friend… Good to see you again. What can I do for you?" I asked after he took off his hat and began to shake the rain off.

He made his way toward me and I could tell by his silence and the expression on his face something was troubling him.

"I was wondering if you got a chance to look at my proposal?" Chucky hesitantly asked and I didn't get the feeling like that's what he really wanted to say.

"Well, actually, I did have time to skim through one of the notebooks. I believe the one that says, ummm… E-FUBU… Something about Education For Us By Us? Tell me a little bit more about this idea," I asked before leaning up against my desk and crossing my arms.

Chucky had my full attention and from what I've read, I honestly thought most of his ideas were big but actually doable.

"Okay, this is what I had in mind. I need to reach a few celebrities. Big ones, I'm talking about those that are worth at least 100 million and better. I read how Magic Johnson had built a chain of movie theaters in urban communities to help with unemployment and I'm sure you heard about how the rapper, Jay-Z from my projects, played a role in that multimillion-dollar arena in downtown Brooklyn. Now, don't get me wrong, they're both beautiful ideas. But I think building more schools would be more beneficial. It will cut down on the class sizes and the curriculum should be geared around the law, black history, and entrepreneurship. It's all in one of my notebooks.

Half of these schools were built over 50 years ago and need some serious upgrading. No disrespect but they got to be black schools, meaning they need to be built and constructed by black folks within the community. We can create our own little union because I don't need to tell you how your folks got a handle on the local unions." Chucky sarcastically stated before briefly pausing for a moment and staring me directly in my eyes.

I understood exactly what he was talking about and while I pondered on how good of an idea it was, Chucky continued, "And we both know that there are enough blacks with the skilled trades getting out of jail that can handle that kind of labor. That's how we help the community. Matching felons with good paying jobs, you feel me?"

I found myself slowly nodding my head yes and I could see the passion in his eyes. He wanted the schools to be named after these wealthy entertainers who helped sponsor the projects. Chucky always had a head on his shoulder, which is why I believe we clicked as teenagers. He had guts and thought outside the box, something I admired about him. The jail had sharpened him up and there was no doubting his sincerity about his ambitions.

I was sure Chucky could see the excitement in my eyes as he continued, "I figured if they can clear people out to build an arena or movie theater, they can do the same with schools.

I think there is a law called Eminent Domain or something like that. I'm sure you know more about this than me."

"Yes, I know exactly what you're talking about which is how the Barclay Arena came about. This sounds great! Listen, got a meeting with some lawyers next Tuesday. Let me shoot your ideas past them and I'll get back to you," I enthusiastically responded.

Chucky was a popular kid in high school and was extremely charismatic. He believed that we could use both of our connections to put together a coalition of black philanthropists to fund the first model. Chucky had me when he explained how much money these people probably donated to other charitable organizations like the Red Cross or local YMCA's. It was a brilliant idea but Chucky needed me to get together with some lawyers that could help find some very good locations and work on the logistics.

"So is there anything else I can do for you?" I asked because it was something in his eyes that told me he had more to say.

"Actually, there is one more thing before I leave." Chucky paused and took a deep breath before speaking again, "I got a nephew who got locked up a couple of days ago. It's also the reason why I'm in the neighborhood. I just came from the court building and they gave him a $20,000 bond. I was wondering if you knew any good lawyers or maybe a bail bondsman I could contact."

I maneuvered my way around my desk and cautiously asked, "What is he locked up for if you don't mind me asking?"

"It's a weapons charge and resisting arrest," Chucky said softly as I fingered through my Rolodex that was sitting on my desk.

"Excuse me but I lost my phone this morning and all my personal contacts. What's his name?" I asked as I dialed the number on the card I'd been looking for.

"His name is Kendell... Kendell Washington."

"Aye, Robbie, this is Mike... Calzone, stop playing. How's the family?" I asked Judge Robert Genaro, a good friend of my father's who'd been sitting on the bench for over 20 years. "Good to hear everything is good with the family... Listen, I need you to help me out with something. There's a young man that was arraigned today named Kendell Washington. What's the situation?"

I could see the look of concern on Chucky's face as I waited for the Judge to pull his name up on the computer. "Okay, this is his third offense but no prior convictions. Listen, he's related to a very close friend of mine. The bail... what can we do?" I asked Robbie while Chucky just stared at me.

"Exactly! That's what I had in mind. You know I love you and I owe you one, Robbie. I'll have Jessica send over some of that 69 Scotch you like. All right... Talk to you soon, buddy." I stated before hanging up.

"So what did he say?" Chucky asked before I could even hang the phone up.

"He's going to see if he can catch him before they send him to Rikers Island. If he can catch him before he gets on the bus, he's going to recall his case and throw out the bail. But you gotta make sure he returns to court."

"What!? Are you kidding me? You got my word on that!" Chucky promised and that was all I needed because he's always been a man of his word.

"Anything else because I gotta run? Ol' lady's waiting for me. Not to mention I gotta stop and pick up another phone," I shared and we both started laughing.

Chucky and I walked out together as he explained an idea he had written down in another one of his black and white notebooks that I've not looked at. He wanted to start a nonprofit organization called The Brooklyn Konnection, to help felons transition into the workforce and Chucky wanted those that were interested to also mentor young troubled men like his nephew to take another path.

I threw my arm around Chucky and curiously asked, "So you say all of these ideas are in one of them notebooks?"

"Absolutely! I'm serious. I need you to take a look at everything I wrote. Someone's gotta grab this problem by the horns. Who knows, you might be the Mayor one day behind this."

"Mayor, huh!?" I responded to my ol' friend who's always thought big. "You know what, Chuck… You're absolutely right. I'll do whatever I can help you get on your feet. You got my word."

"That's all I ask. Because if not… I might be forced to go back to doing what I used to do. And we both know where that's going to take me." Chucky said in a serious tone and he was right.

I felt guilty for many years after Charles went to jail for something I had done. And even though he didn't say it, I did kinda owe him my life. He'd given me his cell phone number and I'd given him my word that I'd call him once his nephew's bail situation was straightened out.

After Chucky left, I went back into my office and grabbed all three notebooks he had given me out of my desk. I threw them in my briefcase and decided to make this my read for the weekend. It was going to be rough but I could see his vision. And there was a part of me that wanted to see my old friend succeed even though the odds were stacked against him.

TRACY

"Hey, girl… Stay strong. If your brother says he's going to take care of it, trust him," I stated to Phyllis again after sitting at a small table inside of the almost empty lounge.

There was a couple sitting in a booth having drinks and a well-dressed man with his back turned toward us sitting at the bar. We'd just got comfortable when a young blonde headed fella with an apron around his waist asked, "Can I get you ladies anything?"

Phyllis sarcastically snapped at the young man, "Can you get my son out of jail?"

"Take it easy. Phyllis! Girl, you need a drink. It'll help ease your mind… Yes, you can get us, um… Two Long Island iced teas… Put an extra shot in them both," I stated as the young man scribbled on a small pad before he spun and left the table.

"I'm calling Shondu to get my boy out now… I'm not gonna let my son sit in a white man's jail another second. I love my brother but come on, Tracy, he just got out of jail. What the fuck can he really do?"

"Come on girl you know your brother… Wait for him to come back and see what he says first," I responded and she ignored my suggestion.

I could hear the phone ringing from the other side of the table and when his voicemail came on she quickly said, "Shondu! Need you to call me back NOW!" Phyllis stated before hanging up. "This nigga never answers his fuckin' phone! Damn, Tracy! Where did I go wrong?"

Phyllis was stressing out and I had no answers since my children's father pretty much raised them. But as a mother, I felt her pain. I worried every day about my sons and would probably be acting the same way she was under the circumstances. I was lost for words when this well-dressed fella that was sitting at the bar turned around and began to approach us, "Hey, ladies, can I join ya'll for a drink?"

When he spoke, my mouth opened wide and when his eyes bulged out of his face, I knew that we both had recognized one another. It was Caesar. I never thought I'd see him again and I immediately responded,

"You bastard! Can't you see my sister is not feeling well?" I sarcastically shot back disgusted at the sight of him.

"Tracy, Tracy, Tracy… No need to be bitchy! I just didn't think whores like you could afford drinks in a place like this," the bastard insulted us as the waiter was returning with our drinks on a small tray.

Phyllis jumped up, her chair fell to the ground and she screamed, "YOU KNOW THIS FUCKIN' CLOWN!"

"Excuse me for mistaking the two of you for ladies," his smartass said before I jumped up and swung at him.

He instinctively raised his arm to block my first blow and backed up a step. Phyllis grabbed one of the drinks off the tray and threw it in his face before flinging the glass in the direction of his head.

"HEY, HEY, HEY! NOT IN HERE!" The waiter shouted as Caesar maneuvered around one of the tables attempting to get away from the both of us but couldn't.

Phyllis was going around the table to the left and I was going around to the right when someone grabbed me from behind.

"TRACY! WHAT THE FUCK IS GOIN' ON!?" Chucky yelled and his masculine voice had me stuck in my tracks.

"I HATE MOTHA FUCKAS LIKE YOU! YOU THINK BECAUSE YOUR WEARING A SUIT AND TIE, MOTHA FUCKA, THAT YOUR SOMEBODY? YOU FUCKING SELL OUT!" Phyllis yelled at Caesar unaware that he used to be my pimp as he tried to wipe the drink off his face and clothes.

Phyllis had moved in on his bitch ass and had gotten close enough to swing at him and he grabbed her by her arms. Caesar had a look in his eyes that I'd seen too many times. Caesar was about to put his backhand slap on Phyllis' face.

"GET YOUR FUCKIN' HANDS OFF ME!" Phyllis yelled just before Chucky turned me loose.

"FUCK HIM UP, CHUCKY!" I screamed at Chucky, who was twice his size and moving swiftly toward Caesar unaware he was the man he'd rescued me from years ago.

"Hey there, take it easy before I call the police," the waiter firmly spoke to Chucky but it was too late.

Chucky had both hands on Caesar, who was tussling with his sister. Another man was coming from around the bar when I yelled at the waiter, "FUCK YOU AND THE POLICE!"

"TRACY! PHYLLIS! BOTH OF YOU CALM THE FUCK DOWN!" Chucky demanded before pushing Caesar's clown ass back and grabbing Phyllis.

Chucky shoved him hard enough that he stumbled up against the tables and chairs. The man that came from behind the bar had jumped in between Chucky and Caesar.

"Chucky, it's Caesar," I cried out.

"Oh shit! You're the nigga that stole my bitch!" Caesar shouted out as the look on his face immediately changed.

"Caesar?" Chucky blurted out loud before mean mugging him. "No need for the police. I'm sure this is all just a misunderstanding. Isn't that right, Mr. Caesar?" Chucky spoke boldly and firmly while slightly tilting his head to the left in awe at the man he'd rescued me from.

"Oh yeah! It's just a misunderstanding. No need for the police," Caesar replied with a dumbfounded expression on his face.

The waiter was picking up chairs and fixing the table but Phyllis and I were still upset. It didn't take long for Chucky to calm us down and speak to the man that had come from behind the bar and turned out to be the owner. He smoothly charmed the owner out of calling the police and letting us stay while Caesar slid his greasy ass out the lounge.

"We'll see each other again, playa! Once a whore, always a whore," Caesar chimed out with his back toward us before laughing and his comments sent chills through my body.

I was stunned at how composed Chucky was because he used to be the type that didn't mind putting his hands on someone who violated his sister, or me, for that matter. Chucky was a kick ass first kind of person and then talk. Brief memories of the night we met and him beating down Caesar crossed my mind until Chucky said, "Come on, ladies, I haven't been home for a hot second and ya'll tryin' to send a brother back already?"

I wasn't sure about Phyllis but his comment had me feeling bad. I placed my hand on his shoulder and whispered, "Not at all, Bae. I'm sorry."

"Who the fuck is Caesar?" Phyllis mumbled out loud after taking a seat at the table.

Chucky shook his head and didn't say a word before locking his eyes directly with mine. He didn't say a word but his fatherly stare spoke volumes. He made me feel like a young girl who had broken curfew.

"He used to be my pimp. That's the guy I told you about," I responded to Phyllis trying to ignore Chucky, who was obviously upset.

I could see the anger in his beautiful brown eyes and knew to get in my lane immediately. Chucky's head turned slowly toward his sister who was still mumbling disrespectful shit that only we could hear when Chucky spoke low and softly, "Listen here, sis… Nephew will be out in a couple of hours. So, let's just relax, have a couple of drinks, and wait for this phone call."

Chucky then sat down and placed his phone down on the table. Phyllis' eyes began to water and her mouth was slightly ajar but nothing was coming out as she glared at her brother as if he was crazy. Phyllis' lips began to tremble as if she was struggling with the words before finally questioning, "WHAT!? What did you do?"

"Yeah, Chucky, where did you go?" I followed behind Phyllis.

"I went to go see an ol' friend. Do you remember Michael? Michael Calzone, the Italian guy that I hung out with sometimes before going to jail. He's the Borough Pres. and he called in a favor for me. He's supposed to call me when Kendell is released." Chucky stated as the waiter returned with fresh drinks.

"Here you go, ma'am, and I'm sorry about the incident but you're going to have to pay for the other drinks," the waiter informed us after apologizing.

"That's cool! I got it," Chucky responded.

"Can I get you anything to drink, sir?" The waiter politely asked Chucky.

"Naaah, I'm good… How much is it for the drinks?"

"The Long Island iced teas are $12 apiece so that would be $48 for these and the two that got wasted," the waiter humbly responded.

"$12 for a Long Island iced tea!?" I enthusiastically asked after he shared the price of a drink that only cost $7 anywhere else.

I was quickly reminded that we were in downtown Brooklyn and on Court Street, where plenty of people with cash lived and worked.

Chucky dug into his pocket and pulled out a $50 bill as if he had forgotten that he'd given me money for the drinks.

"Are you talking about Michael, the white guy that you went to jail for?" Phyllis questioned her brother after he paid for the drinks.

"I didn't go to jail for him, but yes, that one."

Chucky then took his time explaining to Phyllis and me about the phone call his friend had made and the plans he had that was going to change the world. Although, Phyllis and I knew who Michael was, Chucky said very little about him except that he was in Italian guy and his family was connected to the mob.

Chucky figured the less we knew about Michael the better off we'd be, therefore, neither one of us asked too many questions. Chucky had grown the fuck up in prison and this new nigga made my pussy just as wet as the young Chucky that didn't mind snapping a nigga's neck.

CHAPTER
SIX
S H O T S   F I R E D

CHUCKY

I was sitting on the porch of the house where Tracy had been staying. I was sipping on a hot cup of coffee when I heard the door opening. I glanced to the left and noticed my nephew coming out.

"Tracy said you wanted to talk to me," he stated once on the porch.

"Yeah, let me holla at you, nephew. Have a seat." I instructed while my nephew was acting like being in jail was no big deal.

His mother was getting in his ass enough last night after he was released and then thought it was best that he stayed the night with Tracy and me. The boy needed some time off the block and a good talking to.

"Come on, Unc, I'm 23 years old. Don't gimme the father lecture. You already know what it's like on the streets."

"Exactly! That's why you're gonna sit your ass down and listen to what the fuck I got to say! This life and what you want. Think for a second…

Your friend is dead! He's not coming back! That could have easily been you... Boy, if you don't get smart and change, it's going to be you! You hear me?"

"Yeah, I hear you but that's why I gotta get at them nigga's first! Kill or be killed! Isn't that how you live?"

"No... I mean, yes if you're trying to defend yourself. What I used to do and the way I used to think was foolish. That's when I didn't know that the punch was spiked. When I was younger, we used to go to house parties and I drank the punch not realizing that someone spiked it with liquor. It made me do dumb shit!"

"Whatchu, talkin' bout, Unc?"

"I'm talking about life. If you don't educate yourself and gain a little more self-respect for you and the people around you, you are going to do some dumb shit! Something that's going to get you murdered or put in jail for the rest of your life. I'm telling you, boy, the system in this country is not designed for young black boys to be successful men. They profile you, lock you up, and slowly strip away your dignity. Penitentiary is no place for a man let, alone a young boy your age. Stop with this gangsta shit while you can!"

"I'm no gangsta but if you pop off at me, I'm bangin' back at you! Them nigga's started this, Unc! And now I'm gonna finish it just as soon as the sun goes down!"

"You too big for me to keep locked up in the house but I need you to think about something. Think about how your mother is gonna feel if she has to bury you like your friend's mother. When you're dead there is no more nothing boy! No more pussy! No sleeping late! No more nothing! You hear me?" I explained to my nephew before his soul was completely gone.

He had his lips twisted and his head turned away but I continued, "Don't let these crackers or the system break you, boy. I know you grew up in a rough neighborhood. But don't let some fake ass street code like trying to keep it real fuck up your entire life! Don't think that you gotta live by that code forever. I wish I had someone to tell me what I'm telling you when I was your age. You don't have to live this life until you dead or in jail. Listen, I got a friend that's going to help me get you and your mother out the projects. You need a change, a positive one before someone puts a bullet in the back of your head like your friend."

He sucked his teeth and rolled his head around as if what I was saying went in one ear and out the other.

"I'm good because whatever is gonna happen is gonna happen! I'm gonna ride this life until I can't! Everyone has to die someday." He sarcastically responded before I instinctively grabbed him by the neck with my right hand.

I was done being nice with this boy, "BOY, YOU AIN'T EVEN LIVED LIFE YET! YOU COULD BE ANYTHING AND YET, YOU CHOOSE TO BE SOME GANGSTA!? NOT ON MY WATCH! I LOVE YOU AND I WANNA SEE YOU HAVE CHILDREN AND WATCH YOU GET OLD!" I screamed at him, losing my patience.

He was looking ugly and it wasn't until I seen a vain popping up on the side of his temple and his eyes watering that I finally turned him loose. I'd lost it for a moment and after taking a deep breath, I lowered my tone, "I know the young boy's family you're having a beef with. This kid, Prince Maintain... I'm going to see if I could squash this before there's any more bloodshed. You hear me, nephew?"

"Nah, Unc, I don't need you to squash shit! HE KILLED MY MAN! Am I supposed to just forget about that? I ain't no sucker... What would you do if someone killed your friend? Huh, Unc? What would you do?" He barked at me and I had no choice but to be honest.

I placed both hands on his shoulders and looked him dead in the eye before confessing that when I was his age, I felt the same way. I needed him to understand that if I had to do it all over again, I would do things differently. It was that kind of attitude that had me spend most of my adult life in prison. I did my best to make him understand that killing the boy that murdered his friend wasn't going to bring his friend back. That death was final!

My nephew damn sure reminded me of myself. I gave it to him bluntly about the people he called friends and how he would have none once he hits the penitentiary. I told him exactly what I wished someone would have told me 20 years ago. When I was done talking, I grabbed him and gave him a big hug and reassured him that I wanted to grow old with him.

I gave him the lecture that I'd given to plenty of young fellas that I passed in the penitentiary. Most of them had been released and either returned a few years later or was murdered shortly after getting out of jail. A fate that I prayed my nephew didn't put his self or me in.

PRINCE MAINTAIN

"DAMN, Prince! Take it easy, oooh shiiit! Damn, nigga!" CC complained over the smacking sound of my hips slamming up against her ass cheeks.

"Whose pussy is this, bitch?" I questioned as the pleasurable moment was coming to an end.

"AHHHH... Shiiit! It's your pussy...AHHH!" She responded as I picked up the pace of my strokes and released thousands of missiles into her dark abyss.

CC's pussy was soaking wet and my explosion began to simmer down. I was being unusually rough and treating her as if this was my last day.

Some bitch nigga's had a bounty on my head and I was doing my best to put a baby in CC before them nigga's caught me slipping. CC was flat on her stomach and was trying to catch her breath while I laid on top of her back for a moment allowing my soldiers to march up that hill and plant the flag on that chosen egg.

I'd been laying low in her crib for a couple of days until the heat cooled off. Somebody was running their fuckin' mouth because the homicide D's had visited my crib in LG looking for me.

Sweat was drying up on me as I laid on CC's back recuperating from some early morning exercise when my cell phone began to vibrate.

"Well, get off me and get that shit, nigga!" CC grunted before elbowing me in my side.

"Ouch! What the fuck is wrong with you, girl?" I cried out loudly before rolling off of her and reaching for my cell.

"I bet it's one of your lil' bitches from the projects," she snarled at me and crawled out the bed in search for her sexy zebra print thong.

"Wrong, as usual! It's my partner, Smitty. What's good, my dude?" I asked after answering the phone.

"I heard that boy got bailed out yesterday. A little bird told me that the worm is somewhere in Canarsie with is uncle, OG Chucky Washington." Smitty's voice slid out of the phone and into my ear.

"OG Chucky Washington? Word!? They let that motha fucka loose after all he's done? What the fuck? Who told you this?"

The mentioning of his name made me cringe. That nigga killed my pops!

"Yeah, he's back on the streets. I heard he was walking around Marcy the day after that thing we did... you know he's gonna be a problem. Touching his nephew might not be that easy," Smitty continued with concern in his voice.

"Watch your mouth on these jacks but your right. But let me tell you something right now... As a matter of fact, I'll tell you when I see you.

Listen, come check me when the sun goes down. I'm at the honeycomb hideout."

"No doubt... You know we need to step our war game up... I'm low on them shells."

"Yeah, I know. I got a homie in Coney Island that told me to come see him tomorrow. He got what we need and more. He just told me to bring some extra change because he got some big boy toys for sale."

"That's what's up... Fuck wit ya later, shooter," Smitty concluded.

"Pop pop, my nigga," I responded before hanging up.

Smitty was my right-hand man and the only one that knew where CC lived. CC and her mother lived in a brownstone on Remsen Ave. CC was half black and half Italian and was gorgeous as hell with her spoiled ass. Her moms was cool as fuck and her father died before she was born. Her mother's parents were some old-school racists and disowned her when they found out that her baby was mixed. CC's moms is an actress who had been in several movies and gave CC any and everything she wanted.

I'd been fucking with CC for about eight months and, although, she knew I was about that Street life, she loved me to death.

I'd just got off the line with Smitty and was counting some change when she reentered the room, "My mother wants to know if you hungry? She's getting ready to make some breakfast."

I placed my money back in my pants pocket, grabbed her by the hand, and pulled her between my legs as I sat on the edge of the bed in my boxers.

"You're all the breakfast I need, shawty," I stated before motioning for her to sit on my lap. "I just want you to know. If something should ever happen to me that I love you."

"You're scaring me. Whatchu talking about?" She asked.

"I got some beef with these niggas from Marcy and shit might get ugly."

"Ugly how?" CC enthusiastically asked while placing her arm around my neck and playing with my ear.

I then began to tell her what I'd done a couple of days ago. I confessed to her, and only her, how Smitty, Derek, and myself had taken a life.

"Them arrogant niggas from Marcy think they can get away with anything and show their faces as if a nothing happened!" I vented before taking a deep breath and sharing with her the details about that night.

They were about 10 deep and huddled up in a circle shooting dice in front of the corner store around midnight when we peeped them. All three of us were on bicycles in the street dodging oncoming traffic on Nostrand Ave. I glanced over at Smitty, who had been riding up on the sidewalk. Derek and I remained in the street and half way up the block Smitty, with one hand on the handlebars and the other one on his gun, popped off at the crowd first.

K-hooly was on point and the first one to lay eyes on Smitty and after the first shot, quickly dipped up into the store while the other cats scattered. Derek and I jumped off our bikes and started popping off at any one moving. There was one cat trying to make his way across the street but traffic slowed him down and there was nowhere for him to go when Derek and I went to work. We both watched his body drop as cars began to stop while others beeped their horns.

I heard a loud BOOM! When I looked up, K-hooly was standing in front of the store with a pump shotgun in his hand. It was pointed in the direction of Smitty and he was able to cock his joint and get off another shot before I could react. Smitty jumped off his bike and dipped between two cars for shelter.

Derek and I fired back as he stood there as if he was untouchable. We had to duck behind a parked SUV after he pointed the shotgun in our direction and when he popped off, the loud sound combined with the fire coming out the barrel, had us both trying to get off the block.

It wasn't until a couple of niggas came running out the projects with guns in their hands that we decided to clear out. Derek and I turned up the nearest side block and Smitty was halfway up the block. I heard the loud sound of gunfire behind me as I rode through the street. I turned my body and fired two shots back at K-hooly and another cat standing in the middle of the street trying to take our lives.

CC had a strange look on her face and for a moment I thought she was about to cry when I told her how the next day I found out that one of them was dead. By the time I finished telling her about the life I'd taken, it became clear to her why I had been at her house for the last couple of days and only going out at night. It was the only way for me to move at the time because I had to lay low until the smoke cleared.

CC was definitely concerned about someone killing me but I had to remind her that we all have to die sometime. The only thing that I didn't tell her is that the nigga that killed my pops was out of jail and I was at war with his nephew.

ZENOBIA
LATER THAT DAY

The school had just let out and I was standing in front of my house waiting for my daughter to cross the street. She was my youngest of two and seeing her pretty smile running across the street always brought me joy.

"Hey, honey. How was your day, baby?" I asked

"It was fine. Mrs. Chaka gave me 4 stars today."

"4? Why not 5? You know 4 stars is not acceptable, right?" I responded as we climbed up the flight of steps to the brownstone house I'd been living in.

"I know, I'm sorry, mommy," she mumbled softly as I held her hand up the steps.

"Don't worry baby. Mommy is not mad," I stated as my cell phone began to ring.

"Go wash your hands and get yourself a snack before doing your homework," I stated to my baby before answering.

"Yeah, hello," I stated after reading Shondu's name on my caller ID and answering it.

"Hey, what's up? Whatchu doing?"

"Nothing much. Getting ready to help my daughter with some homework, why?"

"I just got off the phone with Chucky... He was asking about you and wanted me to find out where you live and your number."

"Oh really... And?"

"I was calling to give you a heads up that I'm gonna give him your number. Is that cool?"

"Really, nigga!? How you feel about me talking to him?" I sassed back at him knowing that this nigga had caught feelings and was just trying me.

We'd only been fucking for about six months and a bitch really wanted to hear this nigga's response. Niggas ain't shit is what I was thinking when he finally responded just like the nigga I thought he was, "Well, it's not like I'm your man and you're my girl or some shit like that so you can do what you like."

I'm not sure why I expected his greasy ass to say anything different. Therefore, since the motha fucka wanted to play games, I decided to play along with him.

"Sure, give him my number. I would lovvve to talk to Chucky," I stated and there was an awkward silence coming from the other end while a devilish grin grew on my face.

"If you say so," he finally replied and then hung up on me.

I started laughing because he was acting like a typical nigga. Shondu was acting like I was just a piece of pussy so I was going to treat him like he was just a piece of dick. Although, it had been over 20 years since Chucky and I was together, this nigga, Shondu, knew I loved me some Chucky. I would never turn down a conversation or a visit from my baby. But if Shondu wasn't going to tell Chucky about us then neither was I.

I wasn't sure how this was going to play out or if me talking to Chucky was going to touch a nerve in Shondu but the nigga act like he didn't give a fuck so why should I, is what I was thinking when my phone began to ring again. It was a number I didn't know but assumed it was Chucky and when I answered and heard his sexy ass voice for the first time, my pussy instantly began to tingle.

"Hey, Zenobia, this is Chucky." His deep masculine voice hummed through the phone and it made me close my eyes for a moment.

Damn, this nigga sounded sexy as a motha fucka and I could feel the juices between my legs building up. I always dreamed about what I would say the first time we spoke but for some reason he had me feeling like a little girl once again.

"Heeeey, Chucky! Damn, you sound exactly the same. How are you? When did you get out?" I curiously asked because his friend had not mentioned it until today.

I guess Shondu was afraid of us hooking up because Chucky has always been more of a man than he was. I wasn't surprised that Chucky asked to speak to me because of the bond we had. I was one of the only three people that knew what actually happened to King Maintain. A bitch had to keep her mouth shut or else I would've been in jail doing time myself. It was a situation that caused the relationship between me and my sister to be rocky for many years.

"A couple of days ago, and I'm still adjusting. It's good to hear your voice. I need to see you," he stated before getting into his reasons for calling me.

Chucky wanted to see me and was surprised to find out that I still lived in the same house. My parents had passed away and left me the three-story, two family brownstone house on Chauncey Street. Chucky asked me to set up a meeting between him and my sister but I didn't think she would agree because she knew Kaseem and Chucky were good friends. When they found Kaseem and King Maintain bodies, everyone assumed Chucky was there, including my sister, but no one knew for sure.

We'd fallen out behind it and didn't speak to one another for years. Shit was so bad between us that we almost got into a fight at my mother's funeral. She skipped my father's altogether. We just started speaking again a few years ago, but things were never the same. She always blamed me for setting up her baby daddy.

And, although, she was right, it was a secret I was prepared to take to my grave. Asking her to meet with Chucky was like playing with fire but there was nothing I wouldn't do for this man. It would only be a matter of time before he asked me to do something that would probably put me in a situation I couldn't get out of.

CHAPTER
SEVEN
CHUCKY'S PAST DEMONS

CHUCKY

Tracy had to go to work so I rode with her on the A train until I had to get off at Utica Avenue train station. She stayed on and I jumped on the local C train back one stop to Hopkinson, in order to see someone special. I'd talked my nephew into staying in the house until I returned. I needed to go holla at my ex, Zenobia. She had arranged for me to meet with her sister, Shannon, and we both thought it would be a good idea if her sister didn't know that she was meeting with me.

After finding out that Zenobia's nephew was at odds with mine, I decided to take this as my first challenge to squash some beef before more lives were lost. I figured if I could get through to Shannon then maybe she could talk to her son. It was a long shot but no one knew the outcome of the streets like I did.

It felt strange creeping along the steep hill of Hopkinson Ave shortly after 10 PM on a Friday night. There were plenty of new houses where empty lots or burned down buildings used to stand. Zenobia used to be in love with me when we were younger but wanted more than I was able to give her because I was a young hustler that lived on the streets.

Tracy knew all about Zenobia and wasn't quite comfortable with me seeing her but understood that I had to.

Brief memories of the night I killed King Maintain crossed my mind as I passed the spot where he had taken his last breath. I thought about what could have stopped that horrible event from happening but had no answers. I needed one quickly. I needed something positive and convincing to say to Shannon and probably her son.

For some reason, I was nervous when I rang the doorbell while still trying to choose my words in my head correctly. I was admiring the new house next door to Zenobia's when she opened the door with a smile that displayed her pretty gold cap on her front tooth. All I could do was stare because she had put on some weight and cut her hair. She was still looking good but she no longer had the Coke bottle body she had before I went away.

"Hey, Chucky!" She greeted before wrapping both arms around my neck and giving me a strong hug.

I placed my hands around her waist and felt some small love handles before sliding my arms up her back and pulling her close to me. She smelled like a fresh shower and it was the first thing that demanded my attention after noticing the weight she'd gained.

"Hey, Zenobia, look at you… Smelling good and carryin' on," I stated and we both just laughed.

"You know I don't play with my hygiene. But look at you. You no longer the little skinny dude I used to know. Are these muscles!?" Zenobia stated while squeezing on my biceps with both hands.

"Yeah, a little something… And damn, it's good to see you, ma!" I responded still sizing her up.

"It's good to see you, too, after all of these years. Come on in, I was just putting my daughter to bed."

"Daughter, huh? How many kids you got?" I asked entering the house and closing the door behind me.

I followed her into a well-furnished living room which looked completely different as Zenobia told me she had two kids; a 19-year-old daughter that was off in college and an eight-year-old daughter.

When she mentioned having a 19-year-old daughter, I quickly did the math and thoughts of her having my baby crossed my mind. It was brief but I brushed it off. "Hey honey, say hello to my friend, Chucky… Chucky, this is my baby, Tamika," Zenobia stated as her daughter and I exchanged smiles and hellos before Zenobia sent her to bed.

Zenobia had visited me a couple times and then she stopped after she kept running into Tracy. She sent me a letter at least once a month and eventually, that stopped too but I couldn't blame her. I was in jail and she wasn't. I quickly realized that my life was the only one that had been frozen in time. It was the first time since being out of jail that I realized everyone had moved on without me.

"Is there anyone else here besides your daughter?" I asked looking around curiously after her daughter disappeared and left us alone.

"Oh no, just her. And if you're wondering, no, I don't have a man," she continued and we both started laughing. "My sister should be here in a few minutes. Would you like something to drink?"

"Nah, I'm good. I'm just hoping I could get through to your sister before shit gets too crazy!"

"Well, you know she can't stand you. And my sister's attitude has not changed one bit. Good luck with trying to talk to her." Zenobia stated before the doorbell rang.

We both looked at one another as Zenobia was wearing obvious concern on her face. I was hoping I had a chance to talk to her first but it was best I said what I had to, to the both of them at the same time.

I could hear Shannon's mouth from a distance. She was questioning Zenobia's emergency. The last thing I heard was Zenobia saying, "Somebody wants to see you."

Zenobia reappeared first and her sister was right behind her. She paused in the doorway, mouth wide open and eyeballs about to pop out of her skull. "What the? What the fuck is this? Zenobia, is this some kind of fucking joke or something!? I know this ain't why you called me the fuck over here! Un-un, Bitch!"

"Shannon, calm down I need to talk to you."

"Talk to me? About what? How you and your friend killed my baby daddy? I DON'T HAVE SHIT TO SAY TO YOU!" Shannon yelled. "I'M GETTING THE FUCK OUTTA HERE! I know this is NOT what the fuck you called me over here for?" Shannon yelled at her sister.

Zenobia grabbed her with two hands. "Listen, girl. Listen to him! It's about your son!"

"What about my son? He wants to kill him, too… Is that what you wanted to tell me, Chucky? Huh, motha fucka? What, you wanna tell him how you and your friend ambushed his father?" Shannon continued with accusations.

"Listen here, I didn't have anything to do with that," I lied. "Did you know that your son and his friends killed a boy the other day?"

"MY SON IS GONNA KILL YOUR BITCH ASS WHEN I TELL HIM YOU'RE OUT OF JAIL. KEEP MY MOTHA FUCKING SON'S NAME OUT YOUR MOUTH!" Shannon screamed as Zenobia held onto her.

"Listen, that boy was a good friend of my nephew's. I wanted to talk to you about getting them together and trying to save one of, if not both, of their lives. Jail is no place for any man. So, you better listen to what the fuck I got to say before one of them is dead and the other one is in jail."

"FUCK YOU! AND FUCK YOUR NEPHEW! I WISH YOU WAS DEAD!" She screamed at me before she started crying and struggling to get to me.

Zenobia held her tighter just as her daughter stepped into the doorway, "Mommy, what's going on?"

"Nothing, baby, go back upstairs! Auntie Shannon is just a little upset. Go back upstairs and close your door!" Zenobia instructed and her daughter turned and ran off.

"ZENOBIA GET OFF ME!" Shannon screamed as she tussled with her sister.

She had the look of death in her eyes and a dark cloud was in the room when I realized being humble wasn't working so I yelled, "LISTEN SHANNON! I KNOW YOU'RE MAD AT ME BUT I'M SURE YOU LOVE YOUR SON MORE THAN YOU FUCKING HATE ME!"

"I HATE YOU!" Shannon shouted and all I could do was stare at her.

I could feel the pain in her voice when she spoke and knew that I had to continue to be humble, "Okay, I get it! But if there's anyone who knows how these young boys are thinking it's me. I thought about the things I did every day while I was in the mountains LOST! I wish I would have known then what I know now. The system is designed to keep black men like me fucked up and killing one another while women like you are struggling to raise kids on their own! Something has to change and you, a single mother, are the key. You hold your son's life in your hands, Shannon! So, we can do this together, peacefully, so you can watch your son grow old or we can let the streets destroy him like it did his father and me?" I concluded before waiting for her to calm down and give me an answer.

K-HOOLY

My uncle was gone for about an hour and I'd grown a little tired of that righteous shit he'd been kicking all day. Some fuck niggas killed my man and I wasn't going to rest until I returned the favor. Tracy's door locked on its own when I left and made my way to Rockaway Avenue.

My man, Renzo, was waiting for me in a hot car in front of Jimmy Jazz clothing store. He was my dude but I didn't want anyone to know where I've been since getting out of jail. I had to go back to the projects and find out what was going on.

I looked around quickly before jumping in the passenger seat. The car was filled with smoke from a blunt he was smoking on when I got in.

"Yo, let me hit that shit! A nigga's been feigning for a minute." I demanded after getting a whiff of some loud. It had been days since I smoked anything and after taking my first pull, felt like the world was mine.

"Yo, niggas are poppin' off almost every night since that shit happened. I still can't believe my nigga gone." Renzo stated after peeling out.

"Word. Yo, them bitch ass police did me dirty that night. Had my face swollen and all that shit! Fucking pigs!" I stated before taking another pull of the blunt to get my mind off of the bull shit.

"That's fucked up! We got beef with niggas from LG, Tompkins, and the fuckin' police. We should start shooting at them motha fuckas! Shit, we got guns like they got guns." Renzo vented out loud.

"Shit, you already know how I feel about them fuck boys in blue. Yo, let me change the subject real quick. My uncle went to go see some chick that's related to Prince. This nigga trying to get me and him in the same room to squash this shit. My uncle has been gone too fucking long if he thinks some shit like that is gonna happen. He's not the gangsta I heard about. Even though some of the shit he was kicking made sense." I stated before blowing out some smoke.

"He's just trying to keep you alive and out of jail, nigga, don't nobody give a fuck about me like that," Renzo shot back.

"So, when is the funeral?" I finally asked after spotting a cat on the street that looked like the homie.

"His moms cremated him. She's been blaming nigga's in the hood and how she didn't want a bunch of phony motha fuckas at the funeral. So, she says. As a matter of fact, her and your moms were out last night preaching and shit... Talking about we're all brothers and we need to stop killing each other." Renzo continued.

"Word! Mother Shahadah and my moms were out last night?" I curiously asked because it was not like moms to be out on the streets preaching. Now Shahadah, on the other hand, was always out trying to get us to put down the heat and stop selling drugs. We used to hate to see her coming and now it's her son.

"Yeah, they're trying to rally up a couple of mothers and see if they can stop the violence in the hood."

"Can't nobody stop this shit! We live in a kill or be killed world! Just as soon as we put our guns down then what? My moms be trippin'. When we get out to Marcy, make sure you hurry up so I don't run into her. I really don't wanna hear any of that righteous bull shit! Not tonight! And not until we draw blood from one of them niggas," I chimed back before cracking the window and letting out some of the smoke.

Them niggas could run but they couldn't hide. Bed-Stuy wasn't that big so we decided to pick up a couple of burners from his crib and ride around until we laid one of them LG niggas down that tried to kill us.

PRINCE MAINTAIN

"Look, I should be back in about an hour. Gotta go check on moms," I stated to CC who was lying on the bed playing with her phone.

SMACK!

"Did you hear me?" I asked after tapping that ass.

"OUCH! Yeah, I heard you," CC responded while laughing.

This chick knows she loves some social media and sometimes, I think she loves being in other people's business more than me. I slid my hand between the mattress and my hand gripped the 40 Glock while her eyes were glued to her cell. I quickly cocked it, sending one to the chamber before checking to make sure it was on safety.

"Hey, stay with me. Don't go out to LG tonight, please!" CC pleaded after the sound of my gun cocking had gotten her attention. I quickly slid the Glock in my pants waist line before responding, "Come on now! Stop that bull shit! I'm meeting my moms at my aunt's crib. I'm just going to drop her off a few dollars and let her know I'm good. Now gimme a kiss," I requested before leaning in and putting my tongue inside CC's mouth.

While we were kissing, I could feel her right hand on my face and she gracefully stroked my cheek when we finished. CC had a look in her sexy green eyes I'd never seen before so I leaned in and gave her another quick kiss to reassure that everything was going to be okay.

"Don't worry, I'll be back in a few. I promise," I responded before exiting the room.

I was halfway down the steps when I noticed her mother in the living room alone. She was sitting in a recliner reading a book and the sound of me coming down the stairs made her lift her head up and snatch her glasses off.

"Hey, Reggie… Going out this time of night?"

"Yes, Miss Calzone. I'm going to see my mother. I should be back in about an hour. Do you need me to bring anything back?" I asked after reaching the bottom of the stairs.

"No, honey, I'm okay. And I told you to call me Janice." Miss Calzone stated.

She was cool and never questioned what I did. CC's mother was not like the white ladies I'd seen on television. She was really down to earth and wasn't bad looking for an older lady. All she cared about was that I made her daughter happy. I was shaking my head at how fine CC's mother looked when I exited the house hoping CC looked that good when she reached that age.

My boy, Smitty, was parked on the curb in a white wrangler that he purchased a couple weeks ago. My car was stashed in the garage at CC's house because the detectives knew what I was driving and unfortunately, I was the only one they were looking for. My shit was too hot for me to be driving.

"What's good wit ya, boy?" I asked after getting in.

"You already know, fella, eyes and ears on the streets and my back up against the wall as usual." He chanted back before pulling off.

"That's the way we live and that's the way we're gonna die!" I responded as I got comfortable in the passenger seat.

"So, where we going?" Smitty asked while I pulled out a cigar to twist up some burn.

"I need to go check on my mom's first," I stated while emptying the tobacco to the cigar out the window.

"LG?" Smitty asked.

"Nah, nigga! Still too hot for me. She's at my aunt's spot on Chauncy. But look stop at that White Castle up on Utica first. A nigga gonna need a little something to munch on after this shit here," I stated while finishing up the blunt I was working on.

Smitty and I tried to figure out who was talking while we smoked because the police knew too much about me and what happened. Only Smitty, Derek, and I knew all of the details. Smitty was trying to convince me that Derek was a weak link that needed to be dealt with but I wasn't trying to hear that shit at all. Derek was my dude from Fort Greene and came from a family of nothing but gangsters. This nigga's brothers and uncles all had done some time at one point or another. I brushed it off because Smitty had a black hole in his heart for Derek anyway. That's why I wasn't trying to hear what the fuck he was saying.

The drive-through line at White Castle was long, as usual, and it gave us enough time to take a couple pulls of the blunt before placing our order. It was a hangout location for Brooklyn niggas, especially, after a night of partying at the local spots.

It was almost midnight and you would've thought it was a party going on in the parking lot. Cats posted up by their cars in their best, drinking and trying to bag them a little bitch for the night. It was something we'd done plenty of times before but tonight I had other things on my mind.

After eating a couple of burgers, I decided to call moms to let her know that I was on my way. Her cell phone went straight to voicemail. I then called Derek to see what he was getting into.

The shit Smitty was kicking was weighing on my mind and I must admit, had me doubting my man.

Derek was a young dude when we met in Crossroads, a juvenile facility for bad ass kids out in Brownsville. He was straight up gangsta but I still wanted to look him in his eyes and see who he told about what we did.

"Yo, what's up? Where you at?" I asked after he answered.

"I'm chilling. I'm at this little broad's crib on St. Mark's. It's between Bedford and Franklin Ave. Why, what's good?"

"Look, I'm about to go holla at my mom's. I need to put something in your ear. I'm coming to check you in about an hour so we can chop it up, you heard?" I responded.

"No doubt. Just hit me when you're on your way and I'll meet you on the corner of Franklin and Eastern Parkway in front of the Jamaican spot with the burn."

"All right, my nigga," I responded before hanging up.

When I looked up, I noticed that we were passing the Boys and Girls High School on Fulton Street and just a few blocks away from my aunt, Zenobia's, crib.

CHAPTER
EIGHT
E N E M I E S   C R O S S   P A T H S

PHYLLIS

"OKAY, OKAY, OKAY, LADIES! LET'S SETTLE DOWN AND GET THIS MEETING STARTED," I yelled over the crowd of almost a dozen women that actually showed up.

I was more than pleased when Shahadah asked me to help her create an organization of Black women to help fight the growing problem of us losing our precious babies to senseless gun violence. She'd spent the last couple years after converting to Islam trying to educate these young boys in Marcy but after the death of her son, came up with bigger plans. She believed that it was strength in numbers. I agreed because she was not only my friend but I had young boys whose lives I was concerned about.

We handed out fliers all day about this meeting and 11 ladies, besides myself, showed up. It was a small number but a start and once the ladies settled down, I explained the mission before giving Shahadah the floor.

"Okay, ladies I would like to thank you all for coming. We're going to keep this short. Our kids are dying and it's about time we as mothers do something about it!" I started off, standing in the middle of Shahadah's living room floor.

"Yes, girl, it's about time because not a day goes by I don't think about my boys," Mrs. Belmont from the second floor shouted out.

Mrs. Belmont lost two boys to gun violence. Her oldest son, Big Ant, was murdered two years ago at the age of 18. Someone found his head in a box on the bench in the projects and the police found the rest of his body in the Hudson River riddled with bullets. And last winter, someone killed her 17-year-old son. His body was in a green dumpster in Williamsburg with two bullet holes in the back of his head. His murder is still unsolved and it was good to see her at the meeting. She had two other young boys who she was desperately trying to save.

Mrs. Belmont was front and center and I could see the passion on her face when I continued, "We are these babies first line of protection. It's time to start teaching them to BE SMART and not TOUGH! I want grandkids and I want to see my son get old. Unfortunately, it took the loss of my good friend's son for me to finally be sick and tired of being sick and tired. Shahadah and I would like all of you to join our movement to give our children some tough love and educate them about the truth before they are shot down in the streets by the police or someone else."

It was my first time speaking in front of a group of people but something that had to be done. They clapped and cheered me on as I spoke from my heart. I went on for a few more minutes about how I felt about what was going on before passing the floor to Shahadah, who had tears in her eyes.

My girl was sharp! She was very knowledgeable on the hidden race war that is being waged on young black men by old powerful white supremacists. It took a moment for Shahadah to pull herself together before speaking and when she did, everyone listened. Shahadah reminded us about the Jim Crow laws from the 60s and the effect that they were having on our children's success. I was one of the very few people that ever sat down and actually listened to most of the things she had to say after reading a book called "Isis Papers: The Keys to the Colors" by Dr. Francis Cress Weising that she'd recommended. It was a very powerful read that explains some of the reasoning behind white supremacists and the symbolic symbols they have hidden around in plain sight.

Sometimes, I wanted to just have me a drink and talk a little shit but Shahadah never missed an opportunity to share the righteous information she had learned. I knew the ladies were in for something when she took the floor and everyone, including myself, sat in silence as she preached about creating an organization where we began to police our children once again. She wasn't trying to convert any of us into her Islamic religion but open our eyes as well as remind us that as mothers, we are our children's first teachers. Shahadah talked about us breaking the stereotypical traditions that have been taught to our ancestors during the building of this nation and everyone was paying close attention.

Shahadah felt that it was time to tell our children the truth about the things that went on in life behind closed doors. She started by denouncing man-made capitalistic holidays, some which have most people celebrating and practicing pagan rituals. You could hear a mouse pissing on cotton as she explained how Thanksgiving was a slap in the face to the indigenous folks who'd been slaughtered by white Europeans.

"Don't get me wrong, ladies. There is nothing wrong with having a festive dinner with your family but not for the reasons we were taught. And Christmas," Shahadah stated, shaking her head in disgust before breaking it down.

I looked around the room as she went from asking us not to give praise to a holiday that celebrated the slaughter of an entire race to Christmas has nothing to do with Jesus Christ's birthday. I watched the faces on the ladies change as Shahadah continued about each holiday one at a time. Everyone was paying close attention as she did her best to convince everyone in the room that Christmas was a tradition passed down to black slaves without any real explanation. Not realizing that it was meant to drain the free blacks of their financial resources.

Shahadah continued speaking boldly and firm, "It's time for us to question everything that we were taught by our parents. It's not their fault. They were just teaching us what their parents taught them and their parents taught them."

I glanced around after hearing some teeth smacking which gave me the impression that some of the ladies were deeply rooted in the tradition. But after Shahadah played, "The Hidden History of Christmas in Christianity Exposed", a 30-minute video uploaded on Facebook by a gentleman named, Jason Kelly Lamar Martin, the mood in the room had shifted dramatically.

The well-articulated video consisted of Biblical quotes and information that only took a little common sense to truly understand. It was powerful, scary, and definitely enlightening. Before the one-hour meeting was over,

Shahadah wanted us to focus on a couple of things of importance for our next meeting.

First of all, she wanted us to focus on telling our children the truth behind these man made holidays. There was nothing wrong with believing in Jesus but living in a capitalist country run by white supremacists with money and power left it our duty to change the way our kids think and are taught. To basically not be afraid to question how things came about.

Secondly, for us to work on language and self-respect. As our children learn to speak, we should be teaching them the importance of being able to articulate themselves. Communication is important in life and we must teach them early how disrespectful words like "nigga" and "bitch" are to black people. We need to focus on teaching them to respect other people and their property, something we want for ourselves.

And last but not least, the importance of working hard for what you want. Our generation had it rough so most of us believe in providing things for our children we didn't have. But this doesn't teach them how to work hard for the things they need to survive. Our children are growing up expecting things to be given to them and value materialistic things more than their own self-respect.

"It's up to us ladies to lead by example. If you love your kids, then it's time for us to reprogram the next generation with different values," Shahadah concluded and everyone stood up and began clapping.

Shahadah was giving the ladies fliers that had some of the key points of the meeting when someone began to knock on the door. I went to the door and after looking out the peephole of the door, noticed that it was Leticia.

"Hey, girl, what's going on? You just missed the meeting." I stated before noticing the serious look on her face.

"Oh, I'm sorry but I didn't come for the meeting. I came to tell you that I saw your son sitting in a car on the Ave. It looked like him and one of his friends are up to no good and thought that you should know." Leticia stated.

"What!? You must be mistaken because my son is in Canarsie with his Uncle."

"No, he's not. He's on the Ave talking to some young girl."

I thought I'd made it clear to that boy that I didn't want him hanging out around here with them boys he calls friends.

"Thank you, girl, and what you just did is what this meeting was about. Come inside and talk to Shahadah for a minute while I go see what the hell this boy is up to," I stated before screaming at Shahadah that I'd be right back.

Leticia didn't know that what she did is what Shahadah and I wanted as a part of our movement; mothers looking out for other women's children.

We spent too many years caring about our own and not others, like when my mother was younger. We have to raise these children together as a community.

I was hoping that Shahadah was able to get Leticia to join our organization as I rushed to the streets to give my hardheaded ass son some tough love before I had to plan his funeral.

K-HOOLY

"Hey, Cindy... Come here, girl," I hollered out the window at this little slut bucket creeping through the hood as usual.

"Who is that?" She responded from a distance squinting to see who it was.

"It's, Kendell. Come here, girl, and let me holla at you," I demanded. It had been a couple of days since I rubbed ass and Cindy was a chick that all I had to do was get her drunk and smoke something with her to get the panties off. Seeing her ass made me horny as I sat waiting for Renzo to return.

"Hey, K, I thought you were locked up," she stated just before stepping close to the passenger door.

"Stop thinking so much, Shorty... Do it look like I'm locked up?" I shot back at her, making her laugh.

"No, silly! What's going on with you?" She asked.

"Where you going? Come hang out with me for a few," I stated after trying to get a fix on her freak radar.

"I was tryin' to get some weed but these nigga's around here ain't got nothing but that bull shit! A bitch like me need some of that exotic shit!" She boasted.

"I know some dreads on Franklin Ave. with that purp... We can get a sack, a room for the night, and chill. So, what's up?" I asked, licking my lips and playing with her fingers as she leaned in the window.

Cindy fucked a couple of cats from around the way and was usually down for whatever.

"Who are you waiting for?" She asked.

She was hesitant after I told her that I was waiting for Renzo. She didn't like my man because he was a little disrespectful to the ladies but it didn't take long to convince her that he would be on his best behavior.

"Oh, here comes your moms," Cindy stated and had me frantically looking around.

"Damn! Are you serious?" I asked before moms was in my sight and stepping quickly up the Avenue.

"Damn it, man!"

"Hey, Cindy, what's good with you?" Renzo stated as he skated past Cindy and around the front of the car.

"Hey, Renzo," she responded nonchalantly just before he got into the driver's seat.

"Cindy, get in the car. Hurry up!" I demanded just as mom's eyes locked in on mine from half a block away. Cindy was taking her time getting into the backseat as I continued to rush her.

"Here man. Yo, is that your moms?" Renzo stated while passing me a hammer.

I could see the fire in my mother's eyes when I slapped Renzo on the arm and shouted for him to pull off.

"LORENZO, DON'T YOU DARE PULL OFF!" My mother screamed while I tucked the hammer away and demanded that he did.

"NIGGA, PULL THE FUCK OFF!" I screamed again just before Renzo cranked up the car and peeled off.

"How you gonna just pull off on your mother like that?" Cindy instigated from the back.

"KENDELL! GET YOUR ASS BACK OVER HERE. DON'T YOU FUCKIN' PLAY WITH ME!" Mom screamed like a mad lady as I encouraged Renzo to keep it moving.

I was going to have to deal with moms later. There was no way I was going to allow her to embarrass me in front of my man and Cindy. I looked back and noticed her calling someone on her cell phone just before Renzo made a right turn. The feeling of diarrhea was in my stomach at what I had just done. Moms was going to kill me and Renzo so I figured I'd party like tonight was my last night while looking to bring tears to someone's mother's eyes.

CHUCKY

Shannon was obviously upset and wasn't trying to hear anything that I was saying. Zenobia had to pull her into the dining room to calm her down while I thought about my next move. My phone began to ring and when I glanced at it and seen my sister's name, I immediately answered.

"What's good, sis? Can I call you back in a few?"

"I THOUGHT YOU WAS SUPPOSED TO BE WATCHING KENDELL. WHERE ARE YOU?!" My sister yelled through the phone.

"I'm taking care of some business. Why, what's going on?"

Phyllis was cursing and ranting about killing my nephew before the streets did when she saw him. All I could do was shake my head at how hardheaded this boy is while dealing with the disappointment of his actions.

"Okay, sis… Calm down! I'M GONNA FIND HIM." I yelled over her voice and when she started crying, it made me feel like shit!

She didn't have to yell for me to understand the severity of the situation. I promised to get a handle on things and that's what I intended to do at any cost. My sister hung up on me and trying to get through to Shannon was going to have to wait.

"HEY, ZENOBIA, I GOTTA GO," I yelled to her while they went back and forth in the dining room.

Although, I could see them, I was still unable to hear what they were talking about. Zenobia turned and gestured her hand for me to wait a second. I looked at my watch and noticed that it was a few minutes after midnight and I knew that I'd been out just a little too late. There was nothing good out after midnight. It is when the criminal elements are most active.

I decided to text Shondu where I was so that he could scoop me up. I had to find my nephew before he did something stupid. While I was waiting for a response, Zenobia and Shannon joined me in the living room. Shannon's face was twisted and she was tapping her right foot on the floor with her arms folded and she made it her business to be staring at the ceiling when Zenobia began to speak, "Okay, Chucky. We're not making any promises but we will talk to my nephew before things get out of control."

"Hey, Shannon, you're doing the right thing. Listen, we can't go back in time and change the things that we did but it doesn't mean we can't work together to keep the past from repeating itself," I humbly recited.

"Shannon, I'll be right back. Let me walk Chucky out," Zenobia said and Shannon's lips twisted while she sucked her teeth.

"Hey, I gotta find my nephew. My sister called and said that he is out riding around looking to get into some trouble. We'll talk tomorrow." I explained just as I began to receive a text from Shondu.

Be there in 10 minutes.

"Chucky, it was good to see you," Zenobia said while staring directly into my eyes when we got to her front door.

It was an awkward moment, similar to a first date, and I couldn't help but to nervously lean in and give her a kiss. Her soft lips brought back instant memories as she pulled away just in time.

"Good night. You be careful out there," Zenobia whispered before I turned and made my way down the flight of stairs.

I glanced back over my shoulder one last time to see her standing in the doorway. I walked to the corner of Saratoga and Chauncy and decided to wait for Shondu. While I was waiting, I couldn't help but think about that tragic evening that I lost a good friend and took a man's life that looked like me.

It was late and cold when King Maintain bounced down the steps. Shondu and Kaseem were across the street from the house waiting as we planned. When King Maintain chose to go the opposite way, it gave me only a few minutes to run around the block and ambush him coming around the corner. I was jogging with a hammer in my hand, down at my side, when I heard shots poppin' off and knew that the show had started without me.

The different sounds of gunshots are what led me to believe that they were going back and forth. I stopped in my tracks when I heard King Maintain's voice, "COME AND GET ME! YOU BITCH ASS MOTHA FUCKAS!"

I then heard another shot go off when I noticed King Maintain coming around the corner with his back toward me and a gun in each hand. He was firing shots up the block as he backed up. He then turned in my direction and took a couple steps before realizing that the Grim Reaper was standing in front of him. I was dressed in all black with a sweat hood over my head and the barrel of my nigga killa pointing directly at him.

He raised both of his arms and I heard a clicking sound coming from both guns as he squeezed the trigger. My head tilted slightly to the left at the position he was in and it wasn't until he threw one of the guns at me that I pulled the trigger. His other gun fell to the ground when he grabbed his midsection with both hands.

"Oh, shit! You betta kill me, nigga!" King Maintain uttered out loud before I granted him his last wish.

POP! POP! POP!

I began walking toward him and squeezing the trigger with each step I took until I was standing directly over him. His body was trembling and blood was oozing out the side of his mouth and down his chin while I watched him take his last breath. I was completely numb to what was going on around me until Shondu came around the corner with a gun in each hand and shouted, "KASEEM IS HIT. LET'S GET OUTTA HERE!"

Shondu's voice echoed as I read his lips. I was staring at Shondu with my gun pointed down at King Maintain when I fired one more shot that brought me back into reality. Shondu was right, it was time for us to get on the move. It troubled me to leave my good friend bleeding in the street but it was the life we chose. He knew like I knew that it was the risk we took whenever we drew our gun on another man.

The loud sound of music from a white wrangler Jeep snapped me out of the past and brought me back into the moment. It was a couple young boys turning onto Chauncy Street with their music blasting a song I'd never heard before. The smell of weed was coming out of the passenger window as they drove past. The passenger had on a Yankees hat that was down to his eyebrows but I could tell by his head movement that he was watching me as they went by and I kept my eyes on them.

Shondu beeping his horn had broken my stare and he was just in time as the young boys made me think "stick-up kids" because the passenger had been looking at me like I was prey.

"So, what's up with Zenobia?" Shondu asked once I got into the car.

"She's good but her sister, Shannon, didn't take seeing me very well. Zenobia had to calm her down. She eventually convinced her sister into talking to her son before shit gets crazy." I responded while noticing the white Jeep had stopped.

"Oh okay… Did she say anything else?" Shondu's strange question pierced through my ears but my focus was on the two young boys that had gotten out of the Jeep as we drove off into their direction.

I heard him but had no response as I watched the two young men that had just driven past me going up the steps to the house Zenobia lived in.

"A yo, do you think that's King Maintain's son?" I asked Shondu as we cruised past.

Their backs were toward us and I couldn't tell if they were young boys or some nigga's going to check Zenobia.

"I didn't see their faces but trust me, when you see that little nigga, you'll know who he is. That mother fucka looks just like his pops," Shondu informed as we pulled off and headed to Marcy.

I had to find my nephew. I wouldn't be able to live with myself if something happened to that boy. And when he didn't answer his cell for me, I immediately grew concerned that I would probably be too late.

CHAPTER
NINE
A SAUCY NIGHT

MICHAEL

I was sitting in my den going through the last notebook that Chucky had left me. He had some very good ideas and I already figured out ways to help him. Chucky had done his homework while he was in jail because he was extremely detailed. I was truly impressed with his vocabulary and you could tell he put a lot of time and effort into putting it together.

I was taking some personal notes when I heard a soft knock on the door.

"COME ON IN," I yelled from behind my desk.

The double doors opened and I was pleased to see my sister, Janice.

"Aaay, Janice! What brings you by on a Sunday evening?" I asked my baby sister, who seemed to be wearing a look of concern on her face.

"It's about your niece, Chelsea. I need you to help me," my sister responded as she walked toward me.

"Sit down, sis… what seems to be the problem with Chelsea?" I curiously asked.

My baby sister then began to tell me about Chelsea's boyfriend. Chelsea was messing with some young drug dealer that found himself in some trouble. He'd left the house last night and never returned. This morning when Chelsea didn't hear from him, she confided in her mother that he not only killed someone but had a bounty on his head. Janice wanted to know the name of a good lawyer because she believed Chelsea's friend had probably killed someone.

I was hesitant about getting involved but was the only one in the family that Janice could come to for help. My family had never accepted the fact that Janice liked dating black guys and most of them had disowned my baby sister and her child after they found out she was pregnant by one. It caused a great deal of turmoil between our family, who believes that Italians should mix with Italians and blacks should stick with their own kind. It was no problem to do business or even hang out with someone that wasn't Italian but when it came to relationships, mixing races was shunned upon.

"Now, you know there's nothing I wouldn't do for you or my niece. I'm sure I got a couple of numbers I could give you to a good lawyer." I started after she insisted that she was only looking for someone that would give him the best defense possible if he needed. "How is Chelsea?" I asked after finding a couple of numbers for her.

"She's doing okay. She loves a bad boy just like her mother," my sister stated and we both started laughing.

"Hey, I got something to tell you," I said before grabbing my sister's hand.

"What you gotta tell me? You're acting as if it's something serious." She cautiously responded.

I then began to tell her about my visit from Chucky. Janice used to love Chucky and, although, he was my friend the relationship between the two of them was never accepted by my family.

"What are you trying to tell me, Michael? Chucky is out of jail?" Janice asked before snatching her hand away from mine.

"Yes, and I think it's time you told him the truth."

"The truth about what? Chelsea being his daughter? How do I? What do I say after all these years?" Janice questioned.

"I think you should just tell him the truth and Chelsea. She should know that her father is alive and who he is. Both of them need to know. Times have changed. And he might be able to help Chelsea's friend." I suggested.

I showed Janice the books and briefly told her about Chucky's ideas. She was surprised to find out that he was no longer the bad boy she once loved. Janice had become pregnant shortly before Chucky went to jail and since it was a different time, Janice decided not to tell him that she was pregnant. Chelsea was no longer a little girl and after a few more minutes of talking to my sister, she'd finally agreed that it was best that Chelsea got to know her father.

While we were talking, I got a phone call from the Mayor. There was another deadly shooting overnight on Eastern Parkway. A car was sitting at a red light when another car pulled up and opened fired. The deadly shooting left one person dead and another one in critical condition. The Mayor needed me to stand with him tomorrow morning at a press conference and I only agreed after he promised to sit down and discuss Chucky's plans.

ZENOBIA

I'd just gotten off the phone with my oldest daughter, who was in college at the time, when I started to prepare my Sunday dinner. She wasn't coming home for Thanksgiving which was coming up soon but promised to definitely visit during the Christmas holiday. She was adjusting well to her life at Morehouse College and I was missing her like crazy.

I was mixing the spaghetti sauce and pondering on my daughter's achievements when my doorbell rang. I turned the fire down low and hurried to see who it was because I wasn't expecting anyone. A small part of me was hoping that it was Chucky but my wishes were only that when I realized that it was Shondu, Chucky's so-called friend.

Seeing his face made my lips twist and after opening the door, I sarcastically said, "Stopping by without calling now!"

"Yeah, what's up? Is that a problem?" He asked standing in the doorway and being the arrogant nigga that he is.

"I don't have time to play these games. Since when we start poppin' up?" I continued being a smart ass while standing in the doorway with one hand on my hip.

"Well, I'm here now. You're not gonna let me in?" Shondu asked.

I stared at him for a moment and knew that this was a bad idea before rolling my eyes at him and stepping to the side. This nigga knew that we were only fucking but pulled a move that was only designated for a boyfriend. I shouldn't even let his sorry ass in but I didn't want to burn my food arguing with him in the doorway.

He made a loud sniffling sound before saying, "Something smelling good up in here. What are we having for dinner?" Shondu's arrogant ass asked, pretending we were a couple as I followed him into my living room.

"I'm cooking some spaghetti and meatballs and that's the garlic bread in the oven you smell. And let's get this straight. There is no WE!" I made clear before this nigga roughly grabbed me.

"What the fuck is going on with you and Chucky?"

The nigga startled me and I quickly shook loose, "DON'T BE FUCKING HANDLING ME LIKE THAT! AND WHAT THE FUCK DO YOU MEAN? He's your friend, ask him," I yelled before leaving him with my sassy comment and walking off into the kitchen.

Shondu was right behind me yapping and shit about nothing. I could tell this nigga was in his feelings but I didn't have time for his games.

"I'm not sure what your problem is. Didn't you give him my number?"

"Yeah, I wanted to see what was up with the two of you. You still got feelings for that nigga or what?" Shondu reacted jealously and it caught me off guard.

I bust out laughing and he grabbed me by the back of my neck. I could feel the tip of his fingers digging into my neck when I yelled, "YO, GET THE FUCK OFF ME! STOP GRABBIN' ON ME, SHONDU!" I shook loose and turned toward him with my kick-a-motha-<u>fucka's</u>-ass expression all over my face. "Stop acting like you care all of a sudden. Y'all nigga's kill me! It's not like you didn't know how I felt about Chucky from the beginning. Oh, I get it! You're not man enough to tell him what's going on between us, huh? Maybe I should," I threatened Shondu, who knew he didn't want any parts of Chucky.

Chucky might have been talking differently but everyone, including Shondu, knew that Chucky would always have some of that ignorant little boy he used to be inside of him.

"I'm gonna tell him. Just not now," Shondu spoke softly as I finished cooking. I turned off the pots and headed back to the living room with this man shadowing my every move.

"So, who was them nigga's that came to your crib after Chucky left?"

"What the fuck is your problem? Are you stalking me or some shit and why are you interrogating me?" I snapped, angry at his antics.

This motha fucka has stepped all out of his lane and it was time for me to put him back in place, "Listen here. I think it's time for you to leave. You're not my fuckin' man and I don't owe you any explanations!"

He stood there for a moment and I watched his demeanor change right before my eyes. His nose began flaring, he was opening and closing his hand into a fist when I asked again, "Can you please…?"

SMACK!

Before I could finish my statement, I felt the hard rough hand of a slap across my face and I instinctively slapped him back and he grabbed me around my neck with both hands.

"BITCH! I'LL KILL YOU IF YOU EVER PUT YOUR HANDS ON ME AGAIN. YOU HEAR ME, BITCH!?" Shondu screamed at me.

He quickly turned me loose when I began scratching at his face and kicking at him.

"DON'T YOU PUT YOUR FUCKIN' HANDS ON ME, MOTHA FUCKA! WHO THE FUCK DO YOU THINK YOU ARE? GET THE FUCK OUT MY HOUSE! GET THE FUCK OUT!" I continued yelling at him after he backed up to avoid me swinging on him again. He stared at me with a vengeance before I screamed at him again, "GET THE FUCK OUT, SHONDU! NOW!"

He was ignoring me so I turned and hurried to the kitchen. My face was stinging from the slap and I grew angrier which each step that I took.

"You don't wanna get the fuck out! You wanna put your hands on a bitch. I'll show you, motha fucka!" I mumbled out loud to myself as I made my way into the kitchen. I opened the drawer I kept my knives in and rambled through it until I found a small steak knife.

"Put your hands on me again! I continued rambling out loud as I made my way back into the living room with a steak knife gripped tightly in my hand.

Shondu was gone and by the time I made it to my front door, I noticed his bitch ass pulling off. I was trying to catch my breath and calm down but couldn't.

"That motha fucka fucked up!"

I slammed and locked my front door. I was gently biting on my bottom lip and walking back and forth in my living room with the knife still in my hand.

"Fuckin' niggas! I'll fuck who the fuck I wanna! And how the fuck is he going to question what the fuck is going on in my house. Crazy mother fucka! I'll show him crazy!" I continued rambling to no one. I then put the knife down and began to look for my cell.

"So, this nigga wants to put his hands on a bitch, huh? He done fucked with the wrong bitch," I mumbled softly out loud as I waited to hear Chucky's phone ringing.

I quickly hung up before he answered. Not because I was afraid of Shondu but I didn't want to be the reason Chucky went back to jail. A nigga putting his hands on a bitch is one thing Chucky didn't play and

Shondu knew it. I had to calm down and think of another way to get his ass back.

I was on my way to the bathroom to look in the mirror at my face when my phone began to ring. It was Chucky and, although, I'd just called him, I was afraid to answer. I didn't know what to say and really didn't want to put him in the middle of the shit with me and his friend. I ignored the call and seconds later he called right back and I had no choice but to answer.

TRACY

Chucky was on the phone with one of his ol' chicks, Zenobia. I know he was trying to do right by his family and the community but she was the only bitch out of everyone he dealt with that I never liked. Chucky had a soft spot for this bitch and some kind of bond that he always claimed he couldn't talk about. They were kicking it with each other before I met him and since I was never his girl before he went to jail, there was very little I could say.

Chucky had been stressed all day because no one had seen or heard from his nephew since Friday night. Chucky was out all day and night looking for him and his sister, Phyllis, had been calling every hour on the hour to see if Kendell had returned. Even though it was a Sunday, it was my day off so we ordered some Chinese food; something Chucky had been craving since he got out.

I was about to fix a plate for us but he had been in the room on the phone with Zenobia just a little too long. Chucky might have changed but he was still a man and my lady instincts had me tiptoeing through my house to the bedroom. My eyebrows raised near my forehead when I saw the door partially ajar. I slowly eased closer to the door to hear what was going on.

Chucky was pacing back and forth when I heard him saying, "Give me a call after your sister speaks to him again and let me know how he feels. Okay, love you, too, Zenobia."

A funny feeling grew in my stomach with his last comment. I hurried my way back to the kitchen and was putting his plate in the microwave when I heard Chucky's footsteps growing closer.

"So, is everything okay. What did she say?" I asked before checking myself. "I'm sorry. You don't have to tell me. Whatever is going on between the two of you can be between the two of you." I lied.

I said what I thought Chucky wanted to hear and was giving him a chance to tell me what happened on his own.

Chucky's voice was soft when he spoke, "Nah, it wasn't about nothing particular. She did admit that the two dudes I saw Friday night were her nephew and one of his friends. Zenobia's nephew didn't take wanting to meet with me and Kendell too well. Something about them having a beef since they were in junior high school. She said he was furious and that his mother promised to talk to him again one day this week when he cools off."

Chucky was always strong and confident and the worrying expression on his face took away my concerns of him being with Zenobia.

"Hey, what kind of sauce do you want on your food?" I asked hoping to get his mind off his nephew.

"Give me some of that duck sauce… This is what I'm talking about. It's the little shit like this a nigga miss when he's in jail," Chucky responded before breaking a brief smile.

I was placing some duck sauce over his rice when Chucky whispered, "Come here… sit on my lap."

He grabbed my hand and pulled me between his legs and I plopped my fat ass on him without any resistance. "What's the matter?" I reluctantly asked.

"Nothing much… Open your mouth, I'ma feed you. I dreamed about this moment."

"Awww, that's so sweet!" I coed, remembering how romantic Chucky could be.

A man has never offered to feed me before and at that moment, I fell in love all over again. He took his time giving me a fork full of food and then taking one for himself. Chucky had just put some food in his mouth when I leaned in and began to nibble on his ear.

"Whoa, Tracy! Tracy, you're ticklin' me," he stated before laughi is ng.

"Shhh," I whispered softly before gently kissing around his earlobe.

Chucky placed his head up against my chest and I began to use my tongue. I rolled it slowly around the outside of his ear before sticking it inside real quick, making him shiver before moving my lips down to the side of his neck. I could feel Chucky Junior growing underneath me and became excited! I had him and wasn't going to share him with anyone.

Chucky slid his left arm up underneath my legs, placed his right arm on my back, and scooped me up like a baby. I wrapped my arms around his neck and he slowly turned and gently sat me down on the table next to the plate of food we'd been sharing. I pushed the half-eaten plate of food to the side as Chucky started unbuckling my blue jean shorts I only wore around the house.

He was standing in front of me and when he slid my shorts and panties down simultaneously, there was no ignoring the fact that I had become the main course. Chucky had a look in his eyes that confirmed I was the only one he was thinking about.

My legs were dangling off the edge of the table when he wrapped his arms around both my chopsticks forcing me to put my heels on his shoulders. Chucky then placed his face between my legs and confirmed that I was not only the main course but desert. The soft touch of his lips caressing my already wet pussy forced my eyes to close before releasing a soft grunt, "mmm."

Chucky was administering gentle kisses and when his tongue broke through my fortune cookie, he was greeted with some special sauce.

"Mmmm," Chucky softly moaned and it turned me on.

"Yessss… Right there, daddy," I whispered as my breathing began to intensify.

I could feel my chest inhaling and exhaling. The tip of Chucky's nose brushed across my clitoris as he moved his head up and down between my legs. He was giving me long pleasurable licks and when he paused for a moment and put the tip of his tongue directly on my clit, I began to tremble.

"Oh, damn," I whispered just before my body begin to feel weak.

The smacking sound of my tasty sauce made me lose control of my hands. The plate of food hit the floor and Chucky didn't skip a beat.

"Nooo… Chucky stop… Pleeease," I pleaded but didn't mean a word of it.

It wasn't until he wrapped his lips tightly around my clitoris and did this thing with his tongue that I grabbed the back of his head with both hands. I was pleading for him to stop but my body wanted more. I did my best to keep from cumming all over his face but couldn't stop the wet sauce from flowing out. I'd slid halfway across the table until my head began hanging off the edge.

"Stop! I'm gonna fall off the table," I whispered, hoping he would spare me but Chucky only paused for a moment and forcibly slid me toward him.

Chucky brought pure ecstasy to my body and stole my heart all over again.

It wasn't long before we found ourselves lying next to one another on the couch with nothing on. Chucky had been fucking me well and constantly since he'd gotten out of jail. I was drained and my pussy was throbbing when Chucky decided to confide in me about the bond he had with Zenobia. He confessed to killing a man and Zenobia knew.

While we were talking, Chucky's cell phone began to ring. "Hey, get that for me. Hopefully, it's my nephew or my sister."

I jumped up off of him and made my way to the table to get his phone. I wanted to see who was calling him but didn't. Instead, I brought the phone back over to the sofa to Chucky and cuddled up next to him when the phone stopped ringing.

Chucky looked at the phone and squinted before mumbling, "It's Michael… What does he want on a Sunday night?"

Chucky looked at me and I had no answer. "Call him back. He might have some good news for you."

Chucky quickly called him back and I was wrong. Michael had something to tell Chucky about a shooting on Eastern Parkway. He wanted to talk to Chucky first thing in the morning and the lack of information bothered Chucky. Later, Phyllis called and what she had to tell Chucky had blown his mind. He didn't tell me what was going on but I knew it had something to do with his nephew.

He'd been fighting with the demons inside of him to do right but struggled with how he would handle himself if something tragic ever happened to his nephew. A night of blissful lovemaking had turned tragic.

CHAPTER TEN

MEETING OF THE MINDS

MICHAEL
MONDAY MORNING

I was walking with the Mayor and his staff back to his office after the press conference on Brooklyn's most recent murders. There was a shootout between two groups of boys on Eastern Parkway in a predominantly Jewish neighborhood and Rabbi Ashton was applying pressure on the Mayor for some changes.

I followed the Mayor into his office while he barked orders to his secretary to hold his calls while we were in a meeting. His back was toward me when he said, "Michael, talk to me... What's this plan that you have to cut down on the growing violence in your borough?"

"Well, I have an idea. I mean, actually, it's the idea of a friend of mine that I think could work."

"Tell me something because right now anything will do. The press is in my ass, the Rabbi, and the Jewish community is calling for my resignation and Al Sharpton and his National Network is planning some kind of fucking protest one day this week." The Mayor stated after he finally turned to face me while loosening his necktie.

"His name is Charles Washington he should be here shortly. And I'm telling you… If we pull this off, it will make you the Governor. Hell, you might even become the President if this works." I embellished a little.

"Come on, Michael, I hear you talking but you're not saying anything."

"Well, I think it's best if he tells you. We've been going at this problem the wrong way. We've been working on trying to solve it with quick fixes and not focusing on the root. It's going to take some arm-twisting and we might have to get dirty but we will get the results everyone is looking for. Trust me!"

"Trust you, huh? Well, I fucking hope so because I'm fresh out of ideas outside of adding more police to the streets." The Mayor stated before walking over to a small makeshift bar in the corner of his office.

He was pouring a drink as I was receiving a text from Chucky, who was trying to get past security.

"Would you like one?" The Mayor offered.

"Too early in the day for me but this is him texting me now. He's having trouble getting in." I responded while reading the text Chucky had just sent.

"What's his name again?"

"Charles, Charles Washington," I responded as he pressed a button on the intercom that led to his secretary's desk and ordered her to clear him.

"Before we meet with him, I need to let you know that he just got out of prison but he's a good guy. A man of his word and somebody we can trust to do what he says," I stated as the Mayor chugged down a half glass of clear liquor I assumed to be some kind of vodka.

"He's fresh out of PRISON!? For what?" The Mayor asked after shaking a little from the effects of the liquor easing down his throat.

He then reached inside of his pocket and pulled out a little bottle of mouth freshener and shot two quick squirts into his mouth while I briefed him on how Chucky had done some time for a crime that I'd committed.

I was vouching for my friend and putting my career on the line when the Mayor's office intercom began to buzz. He walked over to his desk, pushed a button, and I heard the secretary's voice.

"Mr. Washington is here to see you."

"Send him right in. He better be everything you said, Michael," the Mayor said to me while straightening out his tie.

I was banking on Chucky's charismatic and persuasive abilities to get the Mayor on board. Chucky has a way of charming the socks off you and if that didn't work, was not afraid of trying aggressive tactics when necessary; something I purposely left out of my conversation with the Mayor.

CHUCKY

Last week, I was in a maximum-security prison and now, only a week later, I'm on the opposite side of the door of the New York City Mayor; the man in control of the city and how the money gets disbursed to nonprofit organizations. Michael wanted me to meet him here to help pitch my ideas to the man that could help make it happen.

After notifying the secretary who I was, she picked up the phone and I could only assume she was letting him know that I was waiting. As she spoke to the Mayor, my phone began to ring and I quickly glanced at it and noticed it was my sister, Phyllis. I put the phone on silent and it began vibrating, informing me that I had an incoming text message. I opened the text and before I could read it, heard the secretary requesting that I enter the very prestigious office.

"Hey, Charles, come on in!" Michael stated out loud with a big smile on his face.

He was standing next to the Mayor, a short gray-haired man who was wearing one of the most disingenuous smiles I've ever seen. The Mayor had his hands in his pockets until I got close enough for him to shake my hand.

While we were shaking hands, Michael placed his hand on my back and introduced us, "Charles, this is Mayor Bloomberg... Mayor, this is my good buddy, Charles Washington."

The Mayor was shorter than I'd seen only moments earlier on television as he gave a speech about cleaning up the streets. I was hoping he meant the words he said about being open for ideas and making a difference.

"A pleasure to meet you, Mr. Mayor."

"Well, I'm hoping the pleasure is mine, Mr. Washington. I've heard nothing but good things about you from our friend here," he stated with his face stuck in one position before inviting me to have a seat.

I was a little nervous and felt very uncomfortable being in front of such a powerful man whose expressions I couldn't read. I was like a fish out of the water but knew that this was my moment.

I spent a few minutes discussing The Brooklyn Konnection and how it would benefit people like myself that were just getting out of jail. I insisted that we form a coalition with the union that ran the construction business. It was a good paying job that could help get a felon back on his feet immediately. Most cats in jail were learning most of the skills needed in the business anyway but were coming home with no opportunities.

I watched the expression on his face finally change when I said these men should also be the frontline when building schools, which were the focus of the plan. Schools that would have a boxing facility inside the gym so that young black men could not only relieve the stress of life but learn how to get back to fighting instead of killing one another.

I felt strongly that this generation had lost its ability to handle themselves in one-on-one combat. I explained the importance of schools that focus more on the importance of laws. Not only to follow but how they are made and the politics behind them. The Mayor leaned back in his chair when I mentioned that the school's curriculum should consist of black culture and the history behind the actual building of this country.

I was adamant and passionate when I spoke, "We need to reprogram young black children how to respect themselves and others. Now, don't get me wrong, I'm not trying to alienate or create segregated schools but put together a model that can be followed across the country." I continued speaking boldly just like I rehearsed hundreds of times before in lockup.

I didn't have to convince them that times had changed and it was time for the school system to catch up. The Mayor was nodding his head yes and Michael had grown a huge smile on his face when I continued, "Images of successful people of color and inspirational quotes should be visual throughout the school. And with all this technology, parents should be able to chime into their children's classrooms via Skype to witness some of the things that their children are doing. Children need more oversight and involving the parents when it comes to very troubled ones is a must!" I stated before pausing for a moment.

The Mayor shifted in his chair at my idea before I expressed how I felt about the school system suspending kids.

"Having a child miss a few days of school sets that child back and makes it difficult for them to catch up. And excuse my language but it's the dumbest shit I've ever heard. That doesn't teach kids a lesson. It makes them act up and eventually drop out."

The Mayor's eyes widened at my language as Michael sat there smiling and at times laughing under his breath while I went into details on the plans I'd written down in my notebooks.

My cell phone continued to vibrate during the meeting and when I hesitated for a moment, Michael interjected, "Now, I know what he has planned is a lot but I think he has some really good ideas that we need to consider. Come on now... You just went through this for the Barclay arena. Why not schools?"

"Okay... I've heard enough. Michael, you were right about this guy. I like it! I like your ideas! But how do we get a handle on what's going on now? How do we stop the senseless killing like what happened on Eastern Parkway over the weekend? I have to meet with the parents of the two young men's mother who was murdered while another one is in the hospital fighting for his life. Did you hear about it? It's been all over the news. Two cars riding along Eastern Parkway exchanging gunfire at one another as if this is the Wild Wild West. One dead in each car and another one is in critical condition This has got to stop!" Both Michael and I agreed with the Mayor but I was the only one who had not heard about the tragic shooting.

The Mayor instructed Michael to speak to the secretary to set up another meeting. Michael then agreed to hook me up with someone that was going to turn my notebooks into an official proposal to submit to the Mayor for some grant money. Michael promised I should be up and running in about six months and I was looking forward to it.

"Hey, good job in there! I was very impressed with the way you laid it out. Boy, you still got that charm I tell you," Michael complimented as we left the building.

"I hope so… I got a nephew who is a part of the problem and I'm trying to save him as well."

"Well, I'm with you, Chucky. Because I got a niece named, Chelsea, that loves bad boys and I'd hate for her to get caught up in something she can't get out of. As a matter of fact, Janice came by to see me yesterday and I told her you were out of jail. She said to make sure I tell you hello. As a matter of fact, she wanted me to give you her number."

"Oh, really… How is she?"

"She's doing wonderful! The times have changed my friend."

"So, is she married, seeing somebody, or what?" I curiously asked and was a little surprised that she was a single mom.

"Give her a call and I'm sure she'll tell you everything you need to know," Michael continued while searching through his phone for her number.

After getting Janice's number, I agreed to reach out to Michael before the week was out before he jumped into his Lincoln town and pulled off. He offered me a ride back to Brooklyn but I wanted to take the subway, something I had been enjoying since I got out.

While walking to the train station, I began going through my phone to check the messages and had several missed calls. They were all from my sister, Phyllis, and when I called her back, could barely understand what she was saying as she screamed, yelled, and cried through the phone. She was sobbing while trying to explain how my nephew had been involved in the Eastern Parkway shootout. I was lost for words and for a brief moment had no idea where I was or where I was going but my sister needed me. My nephew had fucked up!

CHAPTER
ELEVEN
TOUGH LOVE

ZENOBIA
SIX DAYS LATER

"Hey there, how is my nephew doing today?" I asked the Jamaican nurse I'd grown familiar with at Kings County hospital.

"Him doing fine. He actually opened his eyes today. His mutter is in wit em now." She responded in her Jamaican lingo with a smile on her face.

It was good to hear that my nephew had opened his eyes after being in the hospital for almost a week. He was shot several times and was in critical condition the first two days he entered the hospital. My sister, Shannon, had not left his side for a moment.

Shannon was playing in his hair when I entered the room, "Hey, girl. I heard he opened his eyes. Oh, My God! Look at you!" I addressed my nephew with a smile on my face after speaking to my sister.

My nephew, Prince, had his eyes open and a small smirk grew on his face when he saw me entering the room with a handful of balloons that had "Get Well Soon" written on them.

"Hey, Auntie Z," he whispered when I stepped closer to his bed, leaned in, and gave him a kiss on the top of his head.

"Save your energy, boy. It's good to see you woke and talking. You scared the hell out of your mother and me! I'm going to put these over in the corner with the rest," I stated before adding the balloons I had to the dozens that were already in the room. My nephew had a lot of friends and the sight of the teddy bears, flowers, and balloons told it all.

"I told him already. I swear this boy is gonna give me a heart attack." My sister responded.

She appeared to be in much better spirits than the first few days when we both were a nervous wreck.

My nephew was alive but the doctors told us that he was lucky not to have been paralyzed. One of the bullets grazed his spine, almost crippling him. Prince was lucky that it wasn't an inch more to the right or he might have been totally paralyzed for the rest of his life.

After visiting for a few minutes, I asked my sister to step out in the hallway for a second. "I love you, baby. Mommy will be right back," my sister whispered as if she was talking to a newborn baby before smothering him with kisses and following me into the hallway.

"Hey, I think you should talk to him again about meeting with Chucky," I spoke softly so that only my sister could hear.

"Not now. Look at my baby." My sister stated.

"Exactly! Look at him. He could have been killed. This might be a good time to have someone talk to him about the streets. If not, next time we will be having this conversation at his gravesite." I boldly spoke my mind to my sister whose eyes began to water.

"Maybe you're right. I'm willing to try anything. I don't know where I went wrong with this boy," my sister responded while wiping her eyes with a tissue.

She finally made the right decision and if Prince was going to change, this was the perfect opportunity to try. Shannon went back in the room to convince my nephew to at least listen to what Chucky had to say while I called him to see if he still wanted to have a one-on-one with Prince. The phone rung several times before a soft feminine voice spoke, "Hello."

"Hello, this is Zenobia. May I please speak to Chucky?" I respectfully asked after a moment of silence to get over the shock that a lady had answered his phone.

"He's in the shower. Can I take a message?" The lady on the other line stated, making it clear that they were close.

"Yes. Can he call me when he gets a chance? It's important."

"Okay. Zenobia? And by the way, this is Tracy, Chucky's girlfriend. I know that y'all are friends but please don't use what's going on between his nephew and yours as an excuse to keep calling him."

Whoa, she knew my name is what ran through my mind after rolling my eyes and choosing my next few words wisely, "Excuse Me! Tracy? That's what you said your name was? I think you are a little out of order, Boo, you don't know me like that!" I quickly responded trying to maintain my cool.

"I'm just saying… he told me all about you and I just wanted to make things clear between us so that there's no misunderstanding." Miss Thing continued with the sarcasm.

"Listen here, little girl! If I wanted Chucky, I would have him. And he told me all about you, too. Are you still doing something strange for your change?" I sarcastically shot back at the bitch that Chucky played captain save a hoe with before going to jail.

I would love to have seen that bitches face. I was sure I'd touched a nerve and just as a foolish grin graced my face, this heifer wasted no time firing back, "Nothing stranger than that thing that got you and your sister not speaking… Boo Boo!"

"Who's that?" Chucky's voice resonated in the background and it stopped me in my tracks.

"Here, it's your friend, the girl whose name starts with a Z," she stated as if she had just forgotten my name that quick.

"Yes, put Chucky on the phone, bitch!" I uttered out loud not knowing if she heard me or not but really didn't give a fuck!

"Hey, what's up?" Chucky asked while I was in my feelings.

"I see you got your little friend screening your calls. You better tell her that I'm not the bitch to be talkin' shit, too!" I expressed to Chucky and he apologized for his little trick.

His deep firm voice brought me instant comfort as I remembered why I was calling. I explained to him how Shannon had agreed to let him talk to Prince. Chucky was aware that my nephew was in the hospital and we all knew that his nephew had something to do with it. The police had no real witnesses but suspected that it was no coincidence that Chucky's nephew's friend was killed the same night Prince was shot and his friend murdered. The police had visited Prince a couple times in order to question him about the incident but he had not gained consciousness until today.

Shannon was having a hard time accepting that her son was a suspect in not one but two murders within the last couple of weeks. There was some kind of gang war going on and we were both surprised to find out that Prince was known on the streets as one of the leaders. We knew he had a lot of friends but didn't know that he was a part of a gang, let alone the boss of one.

I'd just got off the phone with Chucky when my sister returned to the hallway. Prince still didn't want to hear anything that Chucky had to say but Shannon had already made the decision to allow him to visit. She did not want to be visiting her son in jail for the rest of his life or even worse, having to take a trip to the cemetery to drop flowers on his grave every year on his birthday.

CHUCKY

Tracy was upset that Zenobia had been calling me every night and giving me updates on her nephew's condition. It was good to hear that the young boy was doing okay but only half the job was done. I still had to get my nephew to agree to the meeting.

The tension between Tracy and I had escalated since the shooting and Zenobia keeping me posted didn't help. Zenobia's calls usually came shortly before I left the house for a few hours, sometimes I wouldn't return until the morning. I had kept my late-night activities a secret from Tracy for reasons I planned to explain to her later.

This night was no different and, although, Tracy thought I was creeping with Zenobia, I wasn't. After arguing and trying to convince Tracy to trust me, I left. I had been spending the last few days trying to convince my nephew to change his mind. Tracy would not have understood the tactic I was trying and who was actually helping.

ONE HOUR LATER

"Thank you again for letting me do this at your house but I had no other options. This is not how I imagined spending my first few days with you. Did he give you any trouble?" I asked my long-time friend who was giving me the key to the padlock on the door that led to her basement.

"No, not at all and I took him a sandwich to eat around 6 o'clock like you told me and he finally ate it all." My friend responded.

"That's good. This will all be over in a couple of days. I promise," I said to my friend, who shook her head at me before turning and disappearing out of my sight while I took care of the business at hand.

I unlocked the basement door and took my time going down the dark creepy steps. I could hear my nephew's voice faintly as I reached the bottom of the stairs and turned on the light. I didn't respond to his cries while taking my time walking over to the door that led to a laundry room.

There was no lock on the laundry door and when I opened it, I was immediately greeted by a foul odor. My nephew no longer had the appearance of a clean-shaven young boy. Instead, he had the scrappy look of a homeless man and I could tell he was growing tired of sitting in a room where he had to smell his own piss and shit until I arrived to clean out the bucket.

"YO, LET ME THE FUCK OUT OF HERE! WAIT UNTIL MY MOMS FIND OUT WHAT THE FUCK YOU DOING!" My nephew screamed as I closed the door behind me.

"SHUT THE FUCK UP!" I yelled back before continuing. "Had you stayed your punk ass in the house like I asked you to, you wouldn't be in this predicament. Now, I know you don't really know me but let me tell you this. I'm not one of your little friends. I'm gonna save your life one way or another. I tried talking to you and now I got to show you better than I can tell you."

"YOU'RE NOT MY FATHER! YOU CAN'T TELL ME SHIT!" My nephew yelled at me before feeling the wrath of my backhand across his face.

SMACK!

"YO, WHAT THE FUCK!" He screamed at me.

"You think you fuckin' tough? I'm preparing you to spend the rest of your life in jail. How does it feel to be handcuffed? Stripped of your dignity? You like being slapped around like a little bitch and being fed a sandwich every several hours? This is penitentiary! My penitentiary with your young dumb ass!"

Tears came to his eyes and he tried to wipe them away with his left hand because his right hand was handcuffed to a radiator. My nephew's action had cost the life of two more young black men and got another one in the hospital fighting for his life. He was beginning to crack as I gave him a dose of what prison would be like.

"OKAY, I GET IT!"

"WHAT DO YOU GET!" I screamed back at him.

"I DON'T WANNA GO TO JAIL… I GET IT! Now, what else do you want from me!" He asked humbly after lowering his tone and for the first time he let out a loud scream before the crocodile tears rolled down his face.

I'd broken his punk ass just like jail has done to most of the little dudes that visited the penitentiary during my bid thinking they were gangsters. My nephew was not the tough guy his friends thought he was. It only took me less than a week to break him.

"Now, this is what you're gonna do. I'm going to take you to see the boy that you and your friend shot. You're going to give me your word as a man that this beef is going to be squashed. No more gunplay... Do you understand me!?"

"Yes," he mumbled through his tears.

"I can't hear you, son..."

"YES... I give you my word," my nephew cried like the baby he was before I went away.

I felt no mercy because it was about time his ass received some tough love.

"First, you going to call and apologize to your mother. Then I'm going to arrange for you to apologize to that boy's mother. And I'm telling you, boy. If you step out of line when I turn you loose, Lord help the both of us because I'm going back to jail. Don't make me hurt you, boy. You better believe the things you heard about me and know that I love you but you forced my hand. Do we understand one another?"

"Yes, whatever you say. I got it!' He said sniffling and sobbing like a bitch!

I spent another 30 minutes talking to him before emptying the small green bucket that I'd left for him to shit and piss in. The bucket and a roll of toilet tissue were all I left him. I instructed my friend not to move the bucket so that he would know what it was like to be in a jail cell with your toilet bowl stopped up and the correction officers taking their time to fix the problem.

He was pleading for me to let him loose tonight but I figured I'd give him another day or two to really humble his ass. I also wanted to speak to Prince first just to make sure everybody was on the same page. Although, tonight was the first time he shed tears and showed me signs of remorse, the boy still had a little attitude that he needed to shake off.

I ignored his cries to let him loose as I headed back up the stairs and into the house area. When I came up out of the basement, I found my friend sitting in the living room reading a book.

"Hey, love… Again, I'm sorry for any inconvenience," I stated to the only other person I trusted with my life other than Tracy.

"Stop being silly, Chucky… There's nothing I won't do for you. Haven't I proven that to you already?" My friend asked placing the book down and standing up.

"Yes, you have," I stated as she stood in front of me with them beautiful blue eyes.

I grabbed her by the waist and she placed her arms around my neck and our lips locked for a moment. It was a warm embrace I had enjoyed every night I came to check on my nephew and I looked forward to it.

"Hey, let me go before your daughter gets home," I stated before finding myself in a position I didn't want to be in tonight.

"No need to hurry. She's not coming in tonight." My friend said and the message her eyes were sending had been received.

It was at this moment, I would follow her to the bedroom and do some things that would definitely break Tracy's heart if she found out. It was something about the argument Tracy and I had this evening that made me turn the offer down.

"Listen, not tonight. I gotta get back. Tracy already thinks something is going on."

My comment made my friend suck her teeth before responding, "If you say so. I do have a question to ask before you leave. When do you think it's a good time for us to tell my brother that we've been seeing one another.

"Soon, baby… Real soon. Trust me. I have my reasons for not telling him now. I'm sure you understand."

"Yes, I do. I love you, Chucky," she stated before gently stroking my face with the back of her right hand. "There's something I need to tell you."

I then heard Shondu beeping his horn. His timing couldn't have been better because Chucky Junior had woken up and was sending me messages to stay and play.

"Hey listen, I got to go. I promise we'll talk tomorrow and you can tell me whatever it is you have to." I responded before stepping back and staring into the eyes of a lady who apparently had something to say.

It bothered me to lie to Tracy about what I was doing with my nephew but I promised to tell her everything shortly. She'd been acting kind of jealous since I've been home and I didn't think she would be able to handle the truth until I straightened out my nephew. Then and only then would I tell her that I had my nephew handcuffed in the basement of a woman's house that I once loved.

PRINCE MAINTAIN

It felt good to be among the living and I was glad when Auntie Zenobia finally got moms to leave for a moment. I was fucked up but seeing my shawty, CC, by my bedside brought me some comfort. I lost a lot of blood and was feeling weak while my girl used her finger to pull some crust out the corner of my eye.

"I hope you listen to your mother. You scared the hell out of us. Babe, you gotta leave them streets alone." CC stated.

"Come on, I heard enough of that shit from my mother. You don't understand how the streets are!"

"I know the streets killed my father. I never had a chance to meet him because of this thing you call the 'Street life'."

"Yeah, well I don't have any kids," I mumbled in pain.

"Not yet… But you will soon," CC was rubbing her belly and staring directly into my eyes.

"What you talkin' about? Are you pregnant? And you're just telling me?" I spoke out loud and she nodded her head yes.

"I wasn't sure until I went to the doctor three days ago. You're going to be a father and our baby needs you. I need you," CC stated before leaning in and laying a kiss on my lips.

I felt her hand on my stomach next to the bandages but it didn't get my attention until she began to move her hand slowly down my body. Her tongue was in my mouth as I processed what she'd just told me. CC stopped kissing me at the same time her hand grabbed my thermometer. We both felt the temperature rising when she whispered, "What would I do without this?"

"Whoa! I don't know but you better get you a dildo or something until I get better."

"I don't want no fake shit! I want the real thing. Promise me you would at least think about what your mother said. About squashing things with this boy. What is your problem with this boy anyway?" CC finally asked.

The position of CC's hand had me vulnerable and there was nothing I wouldn't do for her. She moved her hand and sat on the bed next to me as I then began to tell her about the man who killed my father, how I despised his family and his nephew most of my life. I couldn't help the way I was feeling inside. I wanted some kind of revenge but CC continued to tell me to let it go. It took some time but she finally got through to me. She was right. I had a baby on the way and had to do things differently.

"Listen, go home and let me think about this," I stated to CC, who had been by my side every night since I entered the hospital.

I knew what it was like to grow up without a father and finding out that she was pregnant had me fucked up.

"I already told my mother I was staying the night with you. I miss talking to you. I miss hearing your voice." CC pleaded. "I don't want to lose you. I'm staying right here until you promise to squash this silly shit!"

"All right, girl. But there is no guarantee that them boys are going to wanna squash things. Blood has already been drawn. Lives have been lost," I spoke softly as we glared into each other's eyes.

CHAPTER
TWELVE
ENOUGH IS ENOUGH

K-HOOLY

"HELP! SOMEBODY HELP! GET ME THE FUCK OUTTA HERE! I screamed and no one responded. My uncle was bona fide crazy! This motha fucka had me locked up in some white bitch laundry room. I lost track of time but knew that I'd had enough. I was ready to get the fuck out of here at any cost. I was beginning to lose my mind. No television, long hours in the dark, and sleeping on a cold floor had broken me. My uncle and some white lady were the only two people that I'd seen in days.

Some white lady would come down every few hours and bring me something to eat but she barely said anything to me. She'd been feeding me bologna and cheese sandwiches or peanut butter and jelly sandwiches, which I can't stand. I'd lost another homie and not being able to attend the funeral was fucking with me something terrible.

I was beginning to talk to myself out loud, "What the fuck is my uncle up to? Who is this white bitch? Where the hell am I? Hold it together, Kendell… Stay strong, nigga… Stay strong!"

I couldn't get the shooting out of my head and every time I closed my eyes, found myself having nightmares about that fatal night.

"Can't keep me down here forever," I mumbled out loud. "What the fuck was that?" I stated after hearing a squeaky sound coming from behind the washing machine. All kinds of things were running through my mind when I heard the squeaky staircase and the sound of footsteps growing louder.

"YO, LET ME THE FUCK OUT OF HERE! YOU GOT IT, UNC'! I PROMISE TO CHANGE." I yelled as the pretty blonde white lady entered the room instead of my uncle.

"I just came to check on you before I go to bed. Are you okay?" She asked as if she was truly concerned.

"Who the fuck is you? And I wanna get the fuck outta here! Please, lady, let me go," I pleaded and she just smiled before speaking.

"Soon my, dear. Real soon, I promise. But you should listen to your uncle. He has a strange way of doing things but he means well," the soft-spoken blonde haired white lady responded without telling me who she was.

"FUCK YOU AND FUCK MY UNCLE! LET ME THE FUCK OUTTA HERE!"

"Your uncle is trying to keep you safe and once you calm down, I'm sure he will let you go. Do you know you look just like your uncle?" She asked and I said nothing.

"Well, I'll be down to check on you in a few hours. Try to relax, which I know is hard to do," the soft-spoken white lady said before leaving.

"Hey, I'm sorry! Please don't leave me down here. Please! At least leave the light on," I pleaded just as she hit the light switch and closed the door behind her.

Tears began to fall down my eyes. My wrist was burning and bleeding from the handcuffs and me trying to get out. I had nothing but a sleeping bag, a roll of toilet tissue, and a green bucket. It was hard for me to sleep because I kept hearing rodents running around. All I could do was think and be angry at the choices I made. After exhausting myself from yelling and crying, thoughts of the night I ran into Prince played over and over in my head.

Cindy and I were coming out of the weed spot after purchasing some green on Franklin Ave and St. Mark's. I had brought a box of magnums, a six pack of Coronas, and some wraps for my purp. A nigga had everything he needed for a pleasurable night with Cindy, my little freak bitch. We were just about to get in the car when I spotted that nigga, Prince, in the passenger seat of a white Wrangler. He must've been talking to the driver because they drove right past without him seeing me.

"Oh shit! Hurry up and get in the car," I instructed Cindy who immediately jumped in the backseat. *"Why you rushin' me? What's the problem?"* Cindy questioned.

"Yo, there go them niggas right there," I hollered at Renzo, who was playing with the radio when I got in.

"Who? Where?"

"That nigga, Prince… They just drove by in a white Wrangler."

"Get the fuck outta here!" Renzo shot back before looking to make sure no cars were coming before he peeled out into the one-way traffic.

I pulled the 40 Glock outta my waist and cocked it. They were out of sight and anger consumed my soul as we sat at a red light at the corner of Eastern Parkway and Franklin Ave wondering where they went.

"Yo… where the fuck did they go?" I asked out loud, looking around for the white Wrangler which had disappeared.

The light was getting ready to turn green when I heard a loud banging sound. The car jerked, snapping my head back and all three of us yelled, "YO, WHAT THE FUCK WAS THAT!?"

Someone had hit us from the back and when we glanced back, immediately noticed that it was the white Wrangler. Renzo made a left turn onto Eastern Parkway and Cindy was in the backseat screaming as I rolled down the window.

I stuck my arm out the open window and fired a couple shots. Pop! Pop! Pop! The Wrangler swerved and Prince returned fire. BOOM! BOOM! BOOM! The fire and the loud noise made me duck back into the vehicle as Renzo ran through a red light. I went to return fire but our vehicle began to swerve out of control. I turned to the front just in time to notice that the car was going up on the sidewalk and it slammed up against a building.

The glass shattered and Cindy was screaming as if she was hit. I was shaking my head trying to gather my thoughts from the crash when I glanced to my left and noticed Renzo slumped over in the driver's seat with a whole in the back of his head. My eyes widened as I looked around to see where Prince was.

I was in a lot of pain when I spotted him walking toward the car. I couldn't see his face but the shit with the long barrel is what my eyes were on. Cindy was screaming when I stuck my arm out the window and started firing at him. POP! POP! POP! POP! POP! POP! POP! I continued until the gun was empty. Prince was lying on the ground trying to crawl back to the car he'd just gotten out of.

The driver of the car that Prince was in was getting out when I quickly leaned over Renzo and opened up the driver's door. He was fucked up so I pushed him out and put the car in reverse. My ears were ringing from Cindy screaming, the gunshots, and the crash. I'd only gotten about three or four blocks when I realized I was unable to see out of the shattered windshield. "COME ON, GIRL. GET THE FUCK OUT. COME ON. LET'S GO," I yelled at Cindy, who was crying hysterically and out of control.

I grabbed her hand and yelled, "CALM THE FUCK DOWN!

Cindy was a mess as we navigated on foot through Crown Heights in the middle of the night to the nearest train station.

I paused for a moment wondering if the police were downstairs. My hands were shaking as the sounds of police cars and ambulances filled the air. Cindy was talking fast and trying to pull herself together when I spotted a gypsy cab. God must've been on my side because we jumped in the cab and was able to get out of the neighborhood with our life and freedom.

I passed the driver two $20 dollar bills to not ask questions and take me to this little hotel out in Sheepshead Bay. I didn't know what to do so after a long weekend of getting high and trying to calm Cindy down. Monday morning, I finally called my moms and told her where I was at and that I'd gotten into some trouble. I didn't give any details but just wanted to let her know that I was good. Later that evening, my Uncle Chucky and Shondu showed up banging on the hotel room door.

When I opened the door, my Uncle punched me directly in the chest and knocked the wind clear out of me. By the time, I caught my breath, there was no misunderstanding that my uncle was in total control. He acted like he had been in this predicament dozens of times before. He'd given me something to drink to help me relax before I woke up in a small room handcuffed to a pipe coming out the wall.

The large boiler in the washer and dryer is what made me realize that I was in someone's basement. My uncle was furious that I didn't stay in the house and called himself teaching me a lesson.

"Oh shit!" I yelled out loud bringing me back into the moment when I felt something crawling on me.

I quickly swiped the small rodent off of me, as I continued yelling and hopping around in one spot trying to chase the rodents back into the walls. These last few days have been pure hell and after all I've been through, couldn't wait to see my uncle to do exactly whatever it was he wanted me to do.

PHYLLIS

"ENOUGH IS ENOUGH! STOP OUR KIDS FROM BEING TOUGH! ENOUGH IS ENOUGH! STOP OUR KIDS FROM BEING TOUGH!" The more than 30 ladies chanted in the small living room at Shahadah's apartment as we wrapped up another meeting.

Renzo, my son's friend's mother had joined our group that we agreed to call MWA (Mothers with Attitudes). She was taking the death of her son much harder than Shahadah who blamed all of her strength on Àllah. She had converted to a Muslim after the death of her twin brother, Monty, which she took extremely hard. We had all seen our share of death but no one could imagine the feeling of losing a twin to suicide.

Shahadah was definitely stronger than everyone else and we had spent the evening teaching the ladies on how to engage their sons that may be involved in a gang. We encouraged them to search their rooms thoroughly for guns and to give their sons random hugs with subtle pat downs every chance they got.

We, as mothers, had turned a blind eye out of love for our children. And I am just as guilty as the rest of them for teaching my son to be tough. I encouraged him to fight back no matter what. I taught him that it was okay to pick up a weapon and defend yourself if you had to, something that has come back to haunt me as well as the ladies in our group.

Shahadah made me realize how our young black children were becoming thugs and gangsters by us. We were teaching our children to behave in a manner that will eventually turn them into criminals. We, as mothers, had finally made a decision to take a stand on taking back control of not only our kids but our community. Most of us were tough ladies that didn't mind confronting a troubled boy's mother. We were going to flat-out start holding them accountable for their children's actions!

We were holding hands in a circle about to engage in a routine prayer before concluding the meeting when we were interrupted by the loud popping sounds of gunshots. Pop! Pop! Pop! Pop! Pop… Clap! Clap! Clap… Boom… Boom!

Instinctively, we all got down low to the ground. "HURRY GIRL! GET AWAY FROM THAT WINDOW!" Shahadah screamed at us as we continued to scramble for cover.

There were several loud popping sounds followed by a couple of loud explosions from a much bigger gun. It was easy to tell that there was more than one gun being fired as I curled up on the floor in front of the sofa with my hands locked tightly behind my head and covering my face with my arms. We all stayed low until the sound of the gunshots finally stopped and that's when Shahadah jumped up and yelled, "OKAY LADIES, ENOUGH IS A DAMN NOUGH! STOP OUR KIDS FROM BEING TOUGH!"

Shahadah looked around the room and yelled, "LET'S GO!" And everyone screamed, "ENOUGH IS ENOUGH!"

It was show-time!

The plan was for all of us to hit the streets to find out who was shooting at who. I glanced around the room and could see the rage in everyone's face as we pulled ourselves together and began to march out of her apartment. Most of us had grown up in Marcy all of our lives and knew most of the people in our community so finding out who was behind the shooting wasn't going to be difficult. We were banking on the people on the streets willingness to talk to us in a moment of gossip before sharing what they knew with the police.

Once we were outside, we all headed in different directions. We would find out as much as we could from different people and meet back at Shahadah's within an hour to determine what was true and which mothers we needed to approach. I was on Park Ave talking to cockeyed Marc when my brother and Shondu pulled up.

Police were everywhere and it didn't take long for Shondu and my brother, Chucky, to realize that there was a shooting shortly before they rolled up.

"Hey, sis, what's up with all the police?" Chucky asked immediately after getting out of the car.

"These young fools are out here shootin' again! This shit is crazy! It's not normal! This shit doesn't go on in no other community!" I complained to my brother, who had the look of concern all over his face. "What's going on with my baby? Is he okay?" I asked, hoping that my brother had a handle on him this time.

"He's good, sis. He's not as tough as I thought he was. The boy just needed a little tough love. Have you seen that girl, Cindy, he was with that night?"

"No, I haven't. I heard she was staying at her grandmother's somewhere in Williamsburg. But fuck her, what about these boys with all of this shooting going on?"

"Hey, sis, these little niggas are just being boys," Shondu foolishly jumped into the conversation.

"Boys being boys? Are you fuckin' kidding me? They're killing each other! We gotta do something about this," I stated as my eyes begin to water and tears drops crawled down my cheeks.

"Hey, sis, take it easy. You and your friends are on the right track. I like what you're doing. Get the mothers involved but know that some of these young boys need a strong hand on their necks." Chucky stated after putting his arm around me attempting to comfort me before he continued. "Look, we're gonna work together. You and your friends work on the mothers and I'll focus on some of these deadbeat niggas. I got a job interview tomorrow with this contractor. Let me get my feet in with these union boys and I should be able to help some of these niggas with some jobs. We got to practice what we preaching."

"I know… I know… I just hope when we find out who was doing the shooting that we could convince their mothers to be tough on them. Lord knows I'm tired of going to funerals and I definitely don't want to bury any of my children. Are you sure everything's okay with my baby?" I asked one more time while wiping the tears out of my eyes.

"He's good, sis. Roof over his head, food, and most of all, staying out of trouble."

"When can I see him? I need to hear his voice," I humbly asked, afraid that something bad could have happened to him. The boy was always in some kind of trouble but my brother reassured me that he was in a safe place and refused to give me any details on how he was handling him. It didn't matter to me as long as my baby wasn't out on the streets acting a fool.

I spent a few more minutes with my brother and Shondu before walking around to find out what else I could about the incident that occurred only moments earlier. Everyone I spoke to told me what they knew, who was involved, and what they thought it was behind.

SHONDU

"Yo, your sister doesn't know what you're doing to Kendell?" I asked before laughing because Chucky was still Chucky deep down inside.

"Nah… She would think I'm being too hard on his ass. She's been pampering and spoiling that little nigga since he was born. That's why he's the way he is now."

"Well, you know he's gonna tell her first chance he gets," I responded.

"So, what… I don't give a fuck? He'll be a man by then," Chucky joked and we both started laughing.

"Hey, yo, I got a question? You don't feel anyway when you're around Shahadah?"

"More now than before but that's water under the bridge," Chucky responded. "That shit haunts me every day. Out of all the shit we did, that one there always bothered me."

"Me, too. I still see his face every time I look at his sister." I said just before Chucky asked me to drop him off at Tracy's crib without saying another word.

Once we were inside of my car, I pumped up the music as Chucky stared out the window, as usual, as if he was seeing the streets for the first time all over again. We vowed to never talk about the things we'd done that were obviously too much for us to repeat. As we headed up Atlantic Avenue, I began to think about this cold night when Chucky and I ran into Demetrius, Shahadah's twin brother, on the evening he lost his life.

Chucky and I were coming out of Black Door, a gambling spot in the back room of a barbershop on Willoughby Ave about a block from the Tompkins projects. It was a hot spot for high rollers from all over Brooklyn and, although, we were teenagers, we had enough money and clout to get in.

Chucky and I were laughing and joking as he counted the $1500 he'd just won. Once in front of the barbershop, Demetrius came staggering around the corner with his head down. It wasn't hard to notice that he was drunk as usual. Neither one of us had seen him in a couple of days, even though he lived in Marcy. Demetrius had been purposely ducking us after fuckin' up some money for like the fifth time. Chucky had a soft spot for *this nigga because his sister was tight with Phyllis. Chucky was rough on anyone else that owed him anything but it was something about this cat I really didn't get and Chucky never explained.*

Chucky always gave him a pass which is why after he fucked up, he'd hidehired for a few days and once he felt Chucky had calmed down, pop back up with a sad story. Chucky would then come up with a way for him to make it up but today would be different.

"Oh, shit! What's up, Chucky? I was just coming to holla at you," Demetrius slurred out of his mouth. You could smell the stench of liquor all over him.

"Demetrius, Demetrius, Demetrius… Where have you been at? I hope you got my doe," Chucky asked before putting his hand on the back of Demetrius' neck.

"Yo, that's what I was coming to tell you. I need a couple more days," Demetrius explained as Chucky marched him up the street.

"Yeah, I know, you're gonna make this shit up for me tonight. Just pull an all-nighter for me to make that money up and we'll be square." Chucky chimed and his compromise had confused me.

Chucky had been talking about kicking his ass on site all day and explaining it to his sister later. Chucky held onto the back of his neck and marched him back to Marcy. He was talking to Demetrius like everything was all good and I must admit the nigga had me fooled but that's the way he moved.

It wasn't until we got in the elevator of Chucky's building that the conversation got strange.

"Yo let's go up on the roof and smoke a blunt first because it's going to be a long night. I'ma stay out with Demetrius until we're square." Chucky humbly stated while patting Demetrius on his back.

"That's cool! That's cool! And I'm sorry again, Chucky. I promise it won't happen again." Demetrius continued as the elevator stopped on the fifth floor.

We got off the elevator and maneuvered up the stairs to the roof and, although, it was winter, it was a spot we went to smoke a blunt from time to time. Kendell was just a baby and Phyllis didn't like Chucky smoking in the crib so the roof was it.

Once we got on the roof, I asked, "You got weed on you?"

Chucky quickly responded, "Nah... It's in the crib."

My eyebrows raised, I was dumbfounded until I heard Chucky's hand across Demetrius' face and I knew he had something else on his mind.

SMACK!

"Oh, shit!" Demetrius cried out after Chucky stung him.

Chucky quickly grabbed him with both hands.

"YOU AIN'T NOTHING BUT A FUCK UP! HOW MANY CHANCES YOU THINK I'M GOING TO KEEP GIVING YOU? YOU GOT NIGGA'S THINKING I'M SWEET. GOT ME LOOKING FOR YOU FOR DAYS LIKE I'M THE AVERAGE NIGGA ON THE BLOCK. DON'T YOU KNOW ME BY NOW NIGGA!?" Chucky screamed at Demetrius, who had grown visually fearful.

I then punched him in the face once I knew that this was a beat down. Demetrius tried to swing back before Chucky and I begin putting the hammers down on him. He fell to the ground and we both began to stomp the fuck out of him as Chucky screamed, "THIS... IS... THE LAST TIME YOU FUCK UP MY BREAD!"

"OKAY! OKAY! OKAY! YOU GOT IT, CHUCKY! CHILL!" Demetrius pleaded as we continued the pounding.

Chucky then grabbed him by both his ankles and yelled, "GRAB THIS NIGGA'S ARMS! YOU HEARD ME! GET HIM!" I heard Chucky and by instinct, I did exactly what he said.

"NO, CHUCKY! I PROMISE TO GET YOU YOUR MONEY! PLEASE! CHUCKY, DON'T DO THIS!" Demetrius screamed and pleaded as he squirmed to the point that we dropped him.

He was crying and snot was bubbling out of his nose but Chucky had a completely different look.

His eyes were bucked wide open and the cold glare in his pupils told me that his body was on the roof with us but his mind was somewhere else. Chucky leaned over Demetrius and punched him real hard in the ribs,

"Stop fuckin' fighting with me! Stop making this harder than it is!" Chucky then looked at me and said, "Help me get this nigga up!"

I grabbed hold to whatever I could and within seconds we had dragged him close to the edge of the roof. We were moving in slow motion as if it was a dream because the moment felt unreal as I helped my friend toss Demetrius off the top of the building.

Chucky was breathing hard from the tussle and when he turned toward me whispered, "You better not tell no fuckin' body. You hear me!?" And I nodded my head yes and followed him off the roof.

"Yo, watch that car!" Chucky screamed as I slammed on the brakes to keep from hitting the car that stopped short in front of me. "Yo, what the fuck is on your mind?"

"My bad! Just thinking, nigga. Your nephew and them young boys. We used to be just like them," I responded.

"Yeah, but we were about money first and foremost," Chucky shot back.

Good thing Chucky said something because I was in deep thought about the night we not only killed the first person in our life but someone we both knew and had grown up with. I glanced over at Chucky and, although, he was talking different and had big plans, I could still see a little bit of the animal he had inside of him when we were younger.

CHAPTER

THIRTEEN

HEADQUARTERS

ONE YEAR LATER - DECEMBER 2, 2014

SHONDU

"Hey, Chucky, your boy looked pissed the fuck off. Is everything good?" I asked when I stepped into his office and caught him staring into space.

It had been a long time since I saw that look on his face and that wicked glare in his eyes.

I was sure he heard me because he slowly shook his head no before he turned and responded, "Our mission of peace and uniting folks is not working. Zenobia's on her way upstate to visit Prince. It's time we take this thing to another level. We have to gain national, no international, attention with our next move. I need you to go see my sister and tell her to get MWA members ready for what we talked about."

"Are you going to be all right? Your buddy Michael looked upset?" I asked knowing that there had been some tension between the two of them.

"Don't you worry about him. Stay focused on the mission at hand. It's bigger than him and I'm sure he realized by now that I used him like him and his family used to me. Fuck his feelings and do what I asked you to do!" Chucky spoke firmly before walking around his desk and opening the top drawer. "And send Tracy in on your way out," he concluded before pulling out a black 45 automatic with a gold handle from the top drawer.

I heard the large and deadly weapon cocking back as I exited the office. "Hey, Trace, Chucky want you in his office," I said to Tracy, who had her back toward me. She turned and as she went to pass me, I grabbed her by the arm, "Talk to him. He's not thinking clearly since they killed Shahadah."

"You just do what he asked you to do. Chucky knows what he's doing." She responded before yanking her arm away from me and walking away.

I watched her disappear into his office and close the door behind her. That bitch is prepared to do anything for Chucky but the crazy shit he was scheming on for the last couple of days has me trying to figure a way out.

MICHAEL

I was exiting the little rat hole spot I helped Chucky get about six months earlier for what I thought was something positive for the neighborhood. Once outside, I glanced back at the bullet holes and realized that my attempt to shake him up had failed. "Is everything okay," Jackie, my driver asked as I reached the car. If my face expressed how I was truly feeling, there was no hiding the disgust from Jackie. "The son of a bitch put his hands on me!" I blurted out as Jackie opened the back door for me. I jumped in ignoring Jackie's question with Ralphie and Luigi right behind me.

Ralphie and Luigi are a couple of friends from my old life and neighborhood who I'd hired to hang around with me after receiving some death threats. Death threats that I knew came from Chucky. The person mentioned things that only Chucky and I had known about. I needed to look in his eyes and know for sure that our friendship was over.

I was turning on the TV when Ralphie asked, "Hey, Mikey, what does this black piece of shit got on you?"

"Enough to put me away. I created a monster and now it's time to put him down." I responded while loosening up my tie.

"So, what's next?" Luigi responded as I began to fix me a glass of brandy.

"Y'all got a good look at him, right?" I asked them both before I continued, "I want him fuckin' dead! Tonight! My old friend leaves me no choice…" I concluded before taking a sip of brandy straight.

"Just him?" Luigi responded.

"No… Kill everyone inside or around that no good rat!" I demanded.

It was a hostile time in New York and the last couple of weeks had been kind of rocky between Chucky and me.

Chucky might be the one that calls the shots in the ghetto but I was the borough Pres. and I called the shots in Brooklyn. He'd been gone for over 20 years but the way people treated him, you would have thought he'd been running this operation a lot longer than six months. Chucky came home acting like a new man, someone that wanted to help educate and uplift black people in his community but rumor has it, he was behind a different level of crime waves, something I promised myself I wouldn't mention to him.

He denied knowing the leader of this new gang that surfaced about six months ago, that call themselves Bitch Killers. They were leaving their calling card mark "BK" at locations after a violent beating of someone white or the burning of a police car and their level of mischief was growing. They were well organized and the police knew very little about them.

They had issued a threat through news media that they were going to start killing cops after what happened this weekend. There was an ugly protest over the weekend and Shahadah, a good friend of Chucky's sister and the leader of MWA (Mothers with Attitudes), was killed by a police officer during the riot. Her and Chucky's sister were close and he made no secret to me about how her death had bothered him.

Ralphie spoke first and broke my chain of thoughts, "So, Mikey, what does this guy got on you?

I slowly turned to Ralphie and softly whispered, "Everything, Ralphie... Everything!"

ZENOBIA

A smile grew on my face when I spotted my nephew coming to the door that led into the visiting area where I'd been waiting. He was looking handsome in his gray jumpsuit and his wavy black hair that he'd cut since being in jail. It was hard to read his stone face as he approached the table I was sitting at.

"Hey, Auntie Z. How's moms?" He asked after sitting down.

"She's doing okay. The doctors say that the chemotherapy is working. She said to tell you that she hopes to see you soon." I responded giving him an update on my sister's condition.

Three months after Prince was arrested for the killing of Kendell's friends, she was diagnosed with breast cancer. It wasn't until she was diagnosed with the illness that my nephew, Prince, had agreed to visit with Chucky. Chucky had shown up the next day to talk to my nephew but the detectives had already arrested him and moved him to a prison infirmary until he got better.

Neither one of them told me what they talked about and I never asked. Chucky had been looking out for my nephew out of guilt for killing his father and not telling on his nephew.

"Tell her I love her and I need her to get better soon," my nephew stated. "I see the cops killed Shahadah. Them fuckin' pigs are out of control. I knew all of that marching and protesting shit wasn't going to change a thing."

"I know, you just focus on doing your time. I do have a message from Chucky. He said that you would know what he's talking about," I stated before leaning in closer to my nephew and whispered what Chucky told me to tell him. It was something about setting the pigeons loose.

"Tell him I said okay. I'll be watching the news. How's my son? I need you to bring him to come visit me next time you come. I need to see him."

"You and CC still not speaking? That girl loves you, why don't you want to see her?" I asked.

"Come on, Auntie Z... I copped out to 12 ½ to 25. They're going to make me do at least two-thirds of that. She shouldn't be worrying and waiting for me for the next 20 years. I just need to see my son. He's the only thing keeping me strong."

My nephew had refused to see CC since they sent him to prison. I agreed to bring his son to visit next time I came and, although, it pained me to see him in jail, it was good to see him thinking clearly for the first time in his life. Prison had calmed him down. He had converted to Islam and was no longer holding a grudge against Chucky. We spoke for a few more minutes before I left feeling like I had lost a part of me.

I was on the bus headed back to the city as the guilt of my role in his father's death began to weigh on me. I began to wonder what my nephew's life would've been like had his father still been alive? If his father lived a different life? Unfortunately, it took my nephew going to prison to grow up and realize that the life on the streets was not kind to anyone. I didn't tell my nephew that my sister was actually dying, which is why she couldn't visit. She wasn't doing well at all and after the long ride back to the city, I finally made up my mind to tell her the truth about what happened to Prince's father. I owed it to her and was prepared to deal with the fallout.

CHUCKY

I was talking to Tracy when I got a phone call from Janice.

"Tracy give me a second, I need to take this call. Let me know when Shondu comes back with my sister." I asked Tracy before she left me to take the call.

"Hey, Chucky, what's going on?" Janice asked in a concerned voice.

"This is not a good time. There's a lot going on."

"My brother just called me and told me to stay away from you and to keep CC away from you. What's going on between the two of you?" Janice asked and it made the hair on the back of my neck stand.

"Exactly what did he say?" I curiously asked knowing my old friend can be vindictive.

Janice then explained what her brother had told her only moments after leaving my office. Michael must be crazy if he thinks that I was going to stay away from my daughter. I had already missed over 20 years of her life because of him.

Janice's phone call concerned me and after talking to her, I couldn't stop thinking about my daughter and the night that I met her. Thoughts of that evening had replaced my evil thoughts for the moment.

I had been out of jail for almost 2 months and Tracy and I had been arguing about Zenobia when I stormed out the house. I found myself walking in the rain and needed someone to talk to and Janice was the only one that came to mind. I didn't know when I called her she was going through something herself.

It didn't take me long to get to her house and what I had on my mind was no longer relevant when she revealed that I was the father of her daughter and how she'd been in her room crying for two days. The news stagnated me and there was an emotional war going on inside of me. It was an overwhelming feeling of joy, betrayal, and confusion all mixed up into one.

"I'm sorry I didn't tell you sooner. But it was a different time. And I've been meaning to tell you since you got out but decided to wait because you had so much going on with your nephew," Janice spoke softly while rubbing the back of my head trying to console me.

I had my eyes closed and my head down trying to process the information when I finally spoke. "Where is she?"

"She's in her room. Up the stairs and the second room on the right. I told her who you were and that you were coming over. I think I upset her even more. Please, Chucky, talk to her." Janice's voice scrambled my thoughts.

Chelsea was beautiful when I entered the room not knowing what I was going to say. She was wrapped up underneath a blanket crying hysterically. After introducing myself, I spent most of the time listening to her vent about her boyfriend who was in jail. I was lost for words when she told me that I was going to be a grandfather. I did my best to console her but really needed someone to console me. It was too much for me in one night so after about an hour, I promised to return the next day.

Things between Tracy and I were rocky that following week as I made it my business to visit and get to know CC a little more. After about two weeks, I discovered that she was having a baby by Prince Maintain. It was something that made me want to reach out to the young man even more. CC and I had grown close to one another in a short time.

It took some time but Tracy finally came around after I convinced her that I wasn't seeing Zenobia. I had no choice but to tell Tracy what I had done with my nephew, who Janice was, and my reasons for keeping it a secret from her. Tracy was with me in the delivery room when my grandson was born and it was a moment I'd never forget. It's also the moment that I realized that what I had to do for my community was even more important than ever.

I couldn't have my grandson growing up in a world that didn't respect young black men. I vowed to use all my resources to make a difference even if it cost me my life!

Thoughts and visions of my grandson being born vanished when Tracy returned.

"Hey, Chucky, here comes your sister and Shondu. Is everything okay?"

"Not really, Tracy. Not really." I humbly responded before telling her what I had on my mind. Then, I had a meeting with the only three people that I felt I could trust. I spent the next 30 minutes explaining to Shondu, my sister, and Tracy how it was time to do something that was going to get the attention of our first black President.

About six months ago, I had Shondu put together a coalition of local drug dealers and gang bangers, with the help of my nephew, for this mission. It took a couple of months to organize them and convince them that it was enough money for everybody and it was time for us to look out for our own. We used the Brooklyn Konnection office and the cats that were fresh out of jail to spread the word.

Shahadah's death had devastated my sister whose pain I truly felt and something drastic had to be done. I managed to organize a group of misfits throughout Brooklyn that were prepared to do whatever I wanted at any time and it was time to turn them pigeons loose.

C H A P T E R

FOURTEEN

T H E   M I S S I O N

MICHAEL

ONE WEEK LATER

I was having a conference call with the Mayor and waiting for Chucky to show up when some loud noises startled me.

POP! POP! POP! POP! POP! BOOM! BOOM... POP! POP! POP!

The muffled sounds of a gun battle going down through my closed-door had demanded my attention. I looked at the closed door just before hearing a painfully loud scream from Jessica before hearing two more shots. I quickly opened the top drawer to my desk but was too late when my office door swung open and Chucky was standing in the doorway pointing in AR 15 at me.

"DON'T DO IT, MICHAEL!" He yelled at me and I was frozen in time. He entered my office quickly with two other men dressed in all black, unlike Chucky, who was dressed in a nice two-piece suit and wearing a pair of shades.

"Chucky, Chucky, Chucky... What the fuck are you doing?" I questioned trying not to display the fear I was feeling at the moment.

"YOU TRIED TO HAVE ME KILLED! YOU KNOW WHAT THIS IS ABOUT!" Chucky yelled back before nodding his head in my direction, triggering his two goons to swiftly move in my direction.

One came to the left of my desk and another one around the right side before I had a chance to get out my gun.

"Come on, Chucky, let's talk. It doesn't have to go down like this," I pleaded as the two men silently maneuvered their selves behind me.

I felt the barrel of both guns pressing up against the back of my head while I slowly slid my hand out of the top drawer.

"Talk about what?" Chucky spoke softly. "I did over 20 years for you. You keep your sister being pregnant from me! And then you try to have me killed! GET THE FUCK UP!" Chucky instructed as he slowly walked toward the front of my desk.

"CHUCKY! COME ON! WHY WOULD I HAVE YOU KILLED?"

"FUCK THE SMALL TALK! I DON'T HAVE THAT MUCH TIME. I THOUGHT YOU WAS MY FRIEND!" Chucky yelled back.

"I..I..I'm sorry you went to jail that night but you doing time wasn't my fault." I stuttered as I stared into the dark black shades that hid the eyes of a man I thought I knew.

"Yes, it was! You or your father set me up! Now tell me why? Why did y'all frame me? You got 60 seconds to tell me the truth. Tell me the truth and I'll make this quick and painless. Lie to me and I'll do you like we've done plenty of people before. I will make your death slow and painful. So, did you have anything to do with it or not? WHO SET ME THE FUCK UP!" Chucky screamed at me.

"OKAY! OKAY! OKAY! My father wasn't happy with Janice being pregnant by you. I swear I didn't know that you were being set up until after you went to jail and there was nothing else I could do. PLEASE, CHUCKY, YOU GOT TO BELIEVE ME!" I pleaded for my life. "Look, I'll give you anything you want. Just name it… I know I owe you. Just tell me what can I do to make this right, my friend," I tried talking my way out of it but Chucky had a look on his face that I had seen many of nights before.

"There's nothing you can do to make up for the 20 years I lost. The time I lost getting to know my daughter! The time I lost with my family! Can you give that back to me, huh! Can you?"

"So, what, you're going to kill me, Chucky? After all we've been through." I tried talking him out of it.

Chucky came around the desk and grabbed me by my jacket.

"No, you're going to tell the world that I was framed. Let's see how you like spending time in jail beating your dick and away from your family." Chucky spoke coldly as he dragged me out of my office.

I could hear sirens from a distance as we entered the reception area. Jessica was lying on the floor motionless behind her desk. I quickly noticed Ralphie and Luigi, my two old friends both on the ground with blood leaking out of their bodies.

"Chucky, look what you did here! YOU'VE LOST YOUR FUCKIN' MIND!" I yelled and it fell on deaf ears.

"You did this! You made this happen! BARRICADE THE DOOR AND CLOSE THE BLINDS," Chucky instructed his two goons after blaming the current situation on me.

They began pushing furniture up against the door as I continued to plead with Chucky that this wasn't the way to go.

"SIT YOUR PUNK ASS DOWN! I'M SURE THE DEATH OF A POLITICIAN WILL GET MORE ATTENTION THAN KILLING A COP!" Chucky yelled before pushing me down into the seat that Jessica had been sitting. "Keep your hands where I could see them," Chucky instructed as he grabbed the phone and began to call someone.

I could tell by his conversation he was talking to somebody from the media. He then passed me the phone.

"Here's your chance to make it up. Tell him the truth about that night. Clear my fucking name. NOW!" Chucky demanded and I had no choice but to tell whoever was on the phone the gory details of the night that I killed a woman that Chucky had done time for.

PHYLLIS

"MOM, QUICK TURN ON THE TELEVISION. HURRY!" I heard my son Kendell yell from his bedroom.

"Tracy pass me the remote control," I said, nervous about what I was going to see.

My brother had been acting strange for the past week. I had not seen or spoken to him since yesterday at Shahadah's funeral. He'd asked Tracy to stay with me for the night because I was falling apart. I just couldn't function after the loss of my friend. She died in my arms and I've been having nightmares about that day ever since.

It bothered me but it did something to my brother. I turned the TV on after Tracy passed me the remote and, although, it was 4:30 in the afternoon, the news came on my screen and our local newscaster, Rafial Gonzales, was on. The words "BREAKING NEWS" were in big letters on the top of the screen as Tracy came to sit by me.

"MOM, IT'S UNCLE CHUCKY!" My son Kendell shouted entering the living room.

"Hush boy! What the fuck is going on?" I mumbled out loud as we all focused on the flat-screen TV hanging on my living room wall.

"We have breaking news folks. 30 minutes ago, I received a call from Michael Calzone, Brooklyn's Borough President and a man that identified his self as Mr. Washington, about the murder of Elizabeth Hernandez, a 34-year-old Hispanic mother of two that was killed over 20 years earlier in a botched robbery attempt.

Apparently, Mr. Washington served time for a crime that Mr. Calzone, our Brooklyn's Borough President, committed. We're still checking the facts of the story but Mr. Calzone has confessed to being the shooter and his father, who was murdered several years ago, had set up and framed his friend. Mr. Washington is allegedly the suspect behind the burning of several churches and liquor stores throughout the city as well as numerous assaults and vandalism.

Hold on a second folks I got some more BREAKING NEWS coming in… Apparently, some inmates in two separate prisons upstate have taken some prison guards hostage. Let me throw it to Sally Munro, a reporter at our sister station in Ossining, New York!"

"Thank you, Rafial Gonzales… We've just found out that a group of inmates are holding hostages inside of the mess hall at Sing Sing penitentiary and Clinton correctional facility, two of New York State's most notorious prisons. We are not clear on who's in charge or if this is connected to the standoff in Brooklyn but we are getting word that they are part of a movement that was triggered by Chucky H. Washington. He's the leader of a notorious gang by the name of Bitch Killers that uses the letters BK to mark their territories which we believe are really the initials of the Brooklyn Konnection, a nonprofit organization that we are now learning was used to hide criminal activity.

Apparently, Mr. Washington has been running the organization for the last six months while using his nonprofit organization, the Brooklyn Konnection, as a front. What started out as a peaceful and positive organization, we are now finding out is behind a wave of crime that's been happening throughout the city for the last week and could possibly be linked to what's going on in the prisons!"

"Oh, My God! No, Chucky!" Tracy blurted out loud as the newscaster continued.

My son sat on the arm of the couch and placed his arm around me as we all continued to listen to the news that was unfolding.

"YES, Chucky!" I cheered, although, I knew my brother was committing suicide.

We watched as the news switched back to the scene on Court Street at Michael's downtown Brooklyn office. There were dozens of police officers surrounding the politician's office and I felt nothing as I watched.

"Oh, My God! They're going to kill him!" Tracy mumbled out loud.

"IT'S A REVOLUTION, TRACY!" I stood up off the sofa and yelled.

"NOT LIKE THIS!" Tracy yelled at me. "DID YOU KNOW HE WAS GOING TO DO THIS? DID YOU?" Tracy screamed at me before my son jumped in between us after I jumped up off the sofa.

"NO! BUT SOMETHING DRASTIC HAD TO BE DONE! THEY KILLED MY FRIEND! THEY'RE KILLING OUR CHILDREN!" I yelled back at Tracy.

"BOTH OF YOU CALM DOWN!" My son, Kendell, screamed out loud before I heard someone banging on my apartment door.

The loud banging had gotten everyone's attention and before we knew it, my door had been pushed in. Several officers dressed in all black riot gear had pushed into my small Marcy apartment.

"GET DOWN! GET DOWN! GET DOWN! EVERYBODY GET ON THE FUCKING GROUND! ON THE GROUND!" Is all we heard as my living room became chaotic.

I could hear my two young boys in the back crying as the police rushed through my apartment.

"WHAT THE FUCK IS THIS? WHAT THE FUCK IS GOING ON?" I yelled as I was tossed to the ground like a criminal and handcuffed.

No one answered my question as I laid on the floor with my hands behind my back. Tracy was to the left of me crying and my son was to the right of me with the look of confusion on his face and water in his eyes.

SHONDU

"LISTEN, ASS HOLE! THIS IS NOT A GAME! I'm gonna step out for a second while you think about if you're going to cooperate or spend the rest of your life in jail with your friends." The old Irish detective yelled after him and his partner had been grilling me for over two hours.

When they left, I remember thinking that Chucky had guided all of us into a suicide mission. He had me set a meeting up between him and five of the most influential gangsters on the streets. Every hood has a nigga that everyone not only respects but fears.

Panama ran most of East Flatbush and was an official gangster. He was on board after Chucky explained how there was more money to be made if he helped cut down on the violence and divided Flatbush into controlled territories, similar to the mob. There was plenty of money for everyone to eat was the message that Chucky was pushing. He convinced Panama that it was the streets against the system. Panama was a cat I met in jail and was not only pleased to meet Chuck but was down for whatever.

We had trouble getting Born, a God body from Brownsville, on board because he had been going to war with a cat name P-O, head of a blood gang that had most of Brownsville under pressure. Unfortunately, one of them had to go and Chucky was really fond of P-O. Chucky saved his life once while they were locked up and P-O owed Chucky.

We already had Bedford-Stuyvesant on lock and after getting the Live

Bunch, a group of hustlers from East New York, onboard, things had been set in motion. There were a few neighborhoods like Coney Island, Redhook, and Bushwick that we just hoped would eventually fall into place. Chucky organized niggas on the streets like the mob.

It was all about getting paper and stacking guns for a moment that Chucky called a Time of Reckoning. Everyone involved had been assaulted or affected by some kind of police brutality. Chucky had everybody stopping by the office as if they were participating in a movement to stop the violence in black communities but was paying dues for a higher cause.

Chucky held regular meetings at the Brooklyn Konnection Headquarters and anyone that didn't cooperate was dealt with immediately and swiftly. No sloppy killings but making young thugs disappear; something Chucky learned from the Italians.

The day after Shahadah was killed, Chucky held a meeting and began to put in motion a plan that would get national attention and hopefully change the systemic racism in the justice and education system. He ordered the burning of churches that we were unable to extort. Chucky believed the local churches were part of the problem because they really didn't kick back to the neighborhood like they were supposed to. Those that didn't benefit the youth in our community were put on a list to be destroyed.

Chucky didn't stop there when he ordered the burning of liquor stores that were not black owned. Our mission of peace had changed and the monster that Chucky had once been had resurfaced. I was on board until he started talking about killing or kidnapping a politician, starting with his friend, Michael Calzone.

It's all Chucky spoke about for the last week after the killing of

Shahadah. The guilt from killing her twin brother had taken its toll on his soul. Chucky's sister, Phyllis, had been encouraging him to do something drastic for days and yesterday when he mentioned running up in his old friend's office, I knew Chucky had gone too far.

A few minutes had gone by before the two detectives returned with an older white lady. She turned out to be the district attorney and had come to make me an offer that I couldn't refuse. I was looking at spending life in jail as I weighed my options. By the time the detectives returned, I had made a decision, one that I was going to have to live with for the rest of my life.

ZENOBIA
SEVERAL HOURS LATER

I was holding my sister's hand, who was slowly slipping away from us. She'd been at this hospice hospital for over a week because there was nothing else the doctors could do for her cancer.

"I'm getting tired," Shannon whispered as I stood next to her bedside holding her hand tightly.

"It's okay, sis, I'm right here with you," I responded as teardrops began to fill my eyes.

"This is her room right here officer," I heard a female's voice say just before two detectives with three uniform officers entered my sister's room.

"Good evening, ma'am, are you Zenobia Grant?" One of the detectives asked me.

"Yes, what's going on? Can't y'all see me with my dying sister." I snapped back.

"Well, you're under arrest," one of the plain clothes detectives mentioned before the three in uniform moved in on me.

"GET THE FUCK OUT OF HERE. FOR WHAT?" I questioned refusing to turn my sister's hand loose.

"For conspiracy to commit murder."

"MURDER! Somebody is making a mistake. Murder who?" I quickly responded.

"Put your hands behind your back, ma'am," a female officer in uniform stated.

"No, y'all made a mistake!" I spoke confused at what was going on.

The three uniform officers began to get rough as I continued to question what was going on.

They had me handcuffed and my body pressed up against the wall as one of the detectives blurted out, "You are under arrest for the conspiracy to commit the murder of Joseph Hawkins."

"I don't know no Joseph Hawkins… WHO THE FUCK IS THAT?" I screamed as one of them began to read me my rights.

"This is a mistake. Shannon, I'll be back as soon as we clear this up. I don't know nobody named Joseph Hawkins!" I continued to say but it didn't matter.

"He went by the name of King Maintain, do you know who we're talking about now?" One of the plain clothes detectives asked and a knot immediately grew in my stomach.

I glanced back at my sister whose eyes were half closed but a small smirk was on her face. "THIS IS A MISTAKE! I DIDN'T HAVE ANYTHING TO DO WITH HIM GETTING KILLED!" I yelled as the detective finished reading me my rights.

They immediately dragged me away from my dying sister and it hurt to know that the last thing she heard was that I was involved in the killing of her son's father, a man she loved.I cried all the way to the precinct while maintaining my innocence and feeling guilty for not being the one to tell my sister. It wasn't until I got to the precinct and spoke to a legal aid lawyer that I found out that Shondu had made a deal with the devil! He told the police everything, including that I had been sending messages back and forth between my nephew and Chucky. They blamed me for the riots that were taking place at Clinton and Sing Sing, where my nephew was being held. My lawyer wanted me to make a deal if I ever wanted to see the streets again.

I was in a nightmare that I couldn't wake up from as my lawyer explained how the district attorney had offered me 12 ½ to 25 as a plea deal or I could take it to trial and get life. All I could think about was my girls and what was going to happen to them while I was in jail. I couldn't stop crying when they finally put me in a holding cell where I had to wait to see the judge.

While I was waiting. Phyllis, Chucky's sister, and Tracy were placed into the cell I was already in. They were just as surprised to see me as I was to see them and it wasn't until they told me what Chucky was up to that I knew we were all in serious trouble. It was at that moment the messages I had been sending to my nephew on behalf of Chucky had become clear. Chucky had used me to get my nephew to create a riot in Sing Sing. I was stunned to find out what was going on since I had not watched television all day, trying to spend the last moments of my sister's life with her.

Tracy and Phyllis seemed to be handling being in jail better than I was. All we could do was sit and wait until we saw the judge, who would eventually tell us what fate had in store for us.

CHUCKY

Several hours had gone by and it was almost time for me to make my point. I was watching what was going on outside Michael's office on a TV he had in the waiting area as the smell of the dead bodies began to circle the room. After hearing the deep voice of a man on a bullhorn screaming for us to put down our guns and come out peacefully was when I decided that it was time to end the standoff.

"What now, Chucky? What is your bright plan now," Michael Calzone taunted me after hanging up the phone. I slapped him across the face with the back of the AR 15 because he was a part of the problem.

"SHUT THE FUCK UP!" I screamed at him as the phone began to ring. I expected it to be some kind of a negotiator but instead it was Janice and her voice brought me back into reality for a moment, "Chucky, please, what are you doing? DON'T DO THIS!"

"Janice. Go home and stay out of this." I spoke as Michael stared at me with murder in his eyes.

"No, Chucky, please! Is my brother okay?" She asked and her voice was trying to melt the cold block of ice sitting in my chest where my heart used to be before the death of Shahadah.

"I HAVE TO DO THIS," I yelled at her even though I knew she would not understand.

"No, you don't. Think about CC. Think about our grandson," Janice threw at me and I held the phone away from my ear. I wanted to hang up but hearing her voice one last time brought me pleasure but reassured what I had to do.

"Think about our grandson, think about our grandson," echoed in my head.

"WHY, CHUCKY? WHY ARE YOU DOING THIS?" She questioned more aggressively and as much as I didn't want to answer, I believed that she deserved to know the truth.

I then told her how her father and brother had set me up for a crime I didn't commit and how I struggled to adapt to society but couldn't. She was quiet as I explained the guilt I felt after Shahadah was murdered. I'd never gotten over killing her twin brother and watching her fight for justice over the last couple of months had me not only admire her but feeling like I owed her.

I watched Shahadah and my sister organize mothers who had lost children to street violence or at the hands of NYPD's trigger-happy police with no results. Shahadah's death was the last straw and that's when I knew that what I was doing was bigger than me and my life. I was doing this for her and my grandson. I was doing this for young black men all across this country. I paused for a moment and Janice pleaded with me not to hurt her brother but my mind was already made up.

I could hear Janice crying when I hung up the phone after refusing to speak to Chelsea, whose voice I heard in the background pleading for me not to hurt her uncle. I then placed the tip of my AR 15 to my old friend's head and asked him one last time, "Did you have anything to do with setting me up?"

"I TOLD YOU IT WAS ALL MY FATHER. I HAD NOTHING TO DO WITH IT!" Michael yelled just before I pulled the trigger.

*   *   *   *   *   *

NEXT DAY

"*Good morning, people. I am Rafial Gonzales, and we're live in front of Brooklyn's Supreme Court building. We've been on top of the story since yesterday. The court room is filled with dozens of people from the media. MWA members are out protesting in support of Charles "Chucky" Washington, who just yesterday murdered four people including the Brooklyn Borough Pres. and former friend, Michael Calzone! Everyone is waiting and watching to see what the media has dubbed the BK 3; Chucky and the two men who killed a politician to make a point. After a 12-hour standoff with NYPD, Chucky H. Washington and his two accomplices had surrendered. If getting national attention was his goal, he's definitely achieved that. Hold on a second, I believe they're bringing them into the courtroom... Yes, they are... We're going live inside to watch the arraignment of the BK 3,*" Rafial Gonzales, the news anchor of NY 1, stated before images of him disappeared and the camera switched to the inside of a crowded courtroom.

CHUCKY

I was taking baby steps as they escorted me into the courtroom with my legs shackled and my hands handcuffed and strapped to a belt around my waist. Panama and P-O were right behind me as the dozens of correction officers surrounded us until we got to the table in front of the judge. We all had separate lawyers but my lawyer was the first and only one to speak, "Good morning, your honor, my name is Lionel Anderson and I'll be representing Chucky H. Washington. Before we proceed, my client would like to make a statement."

"This is just a bail hearing which I'm sure your client will not be getting but I am interested in hearing what he has to say. Motion granted." The middle-age black lady draped in her black and white robe said as she gawked anxiously in our direction.

"First, I would like to apologize to the people whose lives were altered in one way or another by my actions. I've broken many of laws in my life but did 20 years for a crime I didn't commit. I am the product of a system that doesn't work well for young black men and hope that my recent actions, although, tragic has awaken the people in this country up to the pain that most black men like myself feel every day." I stated before looking around the courtroom and quickly blinking after being blinded by the flashes of bulbs coming from the many different cameras before turning back to the judge.

"I am not crazy or mental but fed up and would like to address a particular group of people," I spoke loud and clearly before my lawyer held up a paper that had a letter I had personally written the day after Shahadah's death.

"Dear Russell Simmons, Jay-Z, Dr. Dre, Snoop Dogg, Sean "Puffy" Combs, Michael Jordan, Magic Johnson, and Oprah Winfrey, just to name a few, wealthy and influential people of color.

As a black person living in this country, I am truly confused with why there is not a black coalition amongst those in the $250 million or better club dedicated to investing into building schools in some of the most poverty-stricken neighborhoods.

Money is power and when it's not used correctly then you might as well be a part of the problem. There should be a massive movement of free and modern, elementary, middle, high schools, and colleges being built throughout this nation in minority neighborhoods just like the growth of Walmart.

We are living in a time of technology and great wealth that should be shared amongst all of God's creatures. I put my life on the line by killing not only a politician, but a man I once considered a friend but said nothing as I did time for a crime he committed.

And finally, to those wealthy people of color, I challenge you to continue the fight I started by putting up half of your wealth toward the rebuilding of neighborhoods that were designed to keep people of color in this country constantly fighting a system that was created not to include black people. Thank you and I hope that people like you, Your Honor, and others in power have the guts to stand up for what is right even if you don't agree with my actions." I concluded before the judge remanded me without bail.

I was escorted out of the courtroom with my head up high and hoping that I had got through to those people with money and power that can make a difference. After six months of going back and forth to court, my two comrades and myself were sentenced to life in prison. My old friend, Shondu, was granted immunity to testify at my trial on crimes we had committed, most I had truly forgotten. Zenobia got 6 ½ to 12 years and also testified against me for a shorter sentence and I didn't blame her. My sister and nephew got off on probation because they had absolutely nothing to do with the decisions I made but Tracy was another story.

Tracy refused to testify against me and received 12 ½ to 25 years for conspiracy to commit murder and a host of other charges linked to The Brooklyn Konnection. Her lawyer was unable to convince the judge that she had no idea of what I had planned. As a young man, I ruined a lot of lives for reasons I can't explain. As I sit in solitary confinement at Clinton's Correctional Facility, I have no regrets about the lives I have ruined that got me life in prison, a place I'd grown more comfortable living in than in a society that drained me emotionally before killing my soul just because I was born a **BLACK MAN IN AMERICA!**

THE END

AUTHOR'S

FINAL

THOUGHTS

Thank you for reading and I hope you enjoyed. Please do not take killing a politician, or anyone, to make your point a reality. The message was to kill a politician "FIGURATIVELY" through "VOTING" not through violence. We have to exercise our right to vote not just at the President level but at our lower level as well. We must pay attention to our Mayors, Senators, Councilman, and those closest to the community and hold them accountable for the laws and distribution of funds that continue to keep so many young black men bonded to a system designed to keep them down! Black people must teach our children to be smart not tough! God Bless the next generation! - Kawand S. Crawford

BOOKS BY KAWAND CRAWFORD:

1) Love, Loyalty & Dangerous Games

2) Dangerous Games No Love No Loyalty

3) The Hood Keeper

4) Clients and Their Caregivers

5) Spontaneous Touches and Kisses

6) Spontaneous Touches and Kisses 2

7) Spontaneous Touches and Kisses 3

8) A Bitches Bad Side

9) A Bitches Bad Side 2

10) A Bitches Bad Side 3

11) A Bitches Bad Side 4

12) Summertime Shootings

All Books Are Available On Amazon in Both Paperback and Digital! Don't forget to drop a book review on Amazon and you can follow rhe author on Twitter and Facebook@donkawand... Feel free to visit the authors website at www.donkawand.com

42848113R00113

Made in the USA
Middletown, DE
23 April 2017